Secrets...hopes...dreams...

Welcome to

*Silver *Spires

where
School Friends
are
for ever!

Collect the whole *School Friends* series:

First Term at Silver Spires
Drama at Silver Spires
Rivalry at Silver Spires
Princess at Silver Spires
Secrets at Silver Spires
Star of Silver Spires

Want to know more about *School Friends*?
Check out
www.silverspiresschool.co.uk

Star
of
Silver
Spires

Ann Bryant

USBORNE

For all my piano pupils, past and present!

First published in the UK in 2008 by Usborne Publishing Ltd.,
Usborne House, 83-85 Saffron Hill, London EC1N 8RT, England.
www.usborne.com

Copyright © Ann Bryant, 2008

The right of Ann Bryant to be identified as the author of this work has
been asserted by her in accordance with the Copyright, Designs and
Patents Act, 1988.

Series cover design by Sally Griffin
Cover illustration by Suzanne Sales/New Division

The name Usborne and the devices ♀ ⊕ are Trade Marks of
Usborne Publishing Ltd.

This is a work of fiction. The characters, incidents, and dialogues are
products of the author's imagination and are not to be construed as real. Any
resemblance to actual events or persons, living or dead, is entirely coincidental.

A CIP catalogue record for this book is available from the British Library.

JFMAMJ ASOND/08
ISBN 9780746089590
Printed in Great Britain.

Chapter One

"No, I can't!" I insisted, shaking my head firmly. "Not in a million years!" I added, in case any of my friends hadn't quite got the message.

"But you're so talented, Mia!" said Georgie, my very best friend. "You play the piano like...brilliantly, and you sing like...brilliantly!"

I couldn't help laughing. She looked so funny, throwing her hands in the air dramatically, as only Georgie can.

"And that song you made up is lovely," added Naomi, smiling.

"No, I *really* can't," I repeated. "I'd just be too

scared. I mean *far* too scared!" I folded my arms, and probably looked stubborn and immature. But I couldn't help it. The thought of entering the Silver Spires junior singer/songwriter contest simply filled me with dread.

"I know what you mean about being nervous," said Grace. "I still get nervous every time I do any competitive sport."

I smiled gratefully at Grace. "And this is in front of the whole school," I said quietly. But in my heart I knew that even if it was in front of just the Year Sevens, I'd still never be able to manage it. "I'd...die."

"Which wouldn't be very helpful if you were just about to sing!" said Georgie, looking at me as though I was hopeless.

"Don't pressure her," said Naomi. "Not everyone's as outgoing as you, Georgie!"

I thanked Naomi for that, with my eyes. She's the wise one of the group and I was really pleased that she understood how I felt.

"Well I think Mia needs to be pushed!" said Jess, folding her arms. "She's just too modest!"

The five of us were sitting under one of the trees on the grass behind the main Silver Spires building. Well actually only four of us were sitting under the tree. Georgie was stretched out in the sun. She'd rolled her school skirt over at the waist to make it as short as possible, and she'd tied a knot in her shirt so her stomach could get tanned as well as her legs. It was morning break, and there were loads of other Silver Spires students dotted all over the huge grassy area, some of them lying back sunbathing, others just sitting and chatting. It was the second half of the summer term and also the beginning of the lovely hot weather. It gives me such a nice feeling to be able to look round and know that I'm a part of this beautiful place. Silver Spires is just the best boarding school in the world.

My eyes flicked round my friends and landed on Georgie. "You're getting very pink," I told her. "Did you put suncream on?"

She sighed. "Why did I have to be born with such pale skin? Why can't I be black, like Naomi? Or at least a bit darker than I am, like Grace."

Grace is from Thailand and it's true she's got lovely olive-coloured skin. She sighed and mumbled something about thinking her looks were boring, while Naomi laughed, then turned suddenly serious and stared into the distance. "We should just be happy with what we are, shouldn't we?"

I guessed she was thinking about some of the poor

7

people she's met in Ghana, which is the country she comes from. Naomi is actually a Ghanaian princess, but she hates people knowing that. She feels very lucky to have been born into a wealthy family, and she spends loads of time in the school holidays working for a charity that builds wells in Ghana.

"Well, I'm just as pale as you, Georgie," I quickly said, because Naomi looked sad, and I wanted to bring her back to the here and now.

"And I've got freckles but *I* don't care!" laughed Jess.

"Yes, that's another complaint I've got," Georgie said, sitting up suddenly. "I'd be fine with being pale as long as I had a 'don't care' attitude like you two!"

So then we all laughed, and I felt happy that we'd got away from the subject of the Silver Spires Star contest, because the very thought of singing my own song in front of an audience made me feel quite panicky, and I didn't like my friends trying to push me into it. It was embarrassing and pathetic that I had such a fear of performing in public, especially because music is so important to me and I love playing the piano. But what happened when I was six years old has left a terrible mark on me.

It was my first local music festival and I was playing a piece by Handel. We were all supposed to announce our pieces and say the name of the composer before we played. I remember looking out at all the faces and trying to find Mum and Dad and my baby brother, but Mum's seat was empty. It turned out that she'd had to take my little brother out because he'd started to cry, but I didn't know that at the time and I just felt frightened to see all the faces but no Mum. When I came to announce my piece, in my worried state I couldn't remember the name of the composer, but I knew it reminded me of a doorknob, so that's what I said... "'*Intermezzo*', by Door Knob." And I remember wanting to cry because I didn't understand why people started laughing. And I got so upset then that my fingers didn't seem to work properly and I played the piece terribly and got the worst mark of anyone.

The next year, my teacher tried to persuade me to enter the music festival again but I refused. When I was eight I finally agreed to give it another try, but I felt so sick when I got onto the stage that I had to run off and straight out of the hall, otherwise I would have been sick in front of the whole audience.

After that I never entered one of the town music festivals again, and neither did I play piano in concerts at my primary school, even though my teachers and then my friends tried and tried to persuade me. In the end the teachers gave up because I think Mum must have had a word with them, but my friends wouldn't leave me alone. None of them knew what had happened at the music festivals, and it was far too embarrassing to explain, so I just kept on making excuses that I'd hurt my finger or didn't have a piece ready, or even that I'd lost my music, which all seems ridiculous now.

It was a relief when the Year Six concert at my old school came and went without me having to play in it, but then I came here to Silver Spires and now it looks as though my problems are starting all over again. The real trouble is that I *should* be able to play in public, and I so wish I could. After all, *real* musicians perform in front of audiences and that's what I want to be, more than anything. Music is such a big part of my life that I ought to just make myself get over my fear...only I can't. And even if I managed, by some miracle, to play the piano in public, there are two extra layers of nervousness with this Silver Spires Star competition. You have to write the song yourself, *and* sing it.

I've only written the one song that my friends had heard in my life, and I don't know if it's any good. I wrote it almost exactly a year ago, last May, when I was in Year Six at my primary school. I was feeling really sad at the time because I knew I was going to be coming here to Silver Spires Boarding School in September, and although I was excited in some ways, I also knew I'd really miss Mum and Dad and my little brother. And I was right, because I did get homesick during the first few weeks, and I even found it hard coming back to school after the holidays for this third term. But I'm lucky because I've got the best, best friend in the world.

Georgie and I met on the induction day and then had a brilliant surprise on our first day at Silver Spires when we found we'd been put in the same dorm. The dorm is called Amethyst and it's in Hazeldean boarding house, which we naturally think is the best boarding house. There are six of us in the dorm – me, Georgie, Naomi, Katy, Grace and Jess, and we spend loads of time together. Like right now, because Katy was rushing over to us, looking very excited.

"Hiya!"

"Where've you been?" Naomi asked her.

"Bumped into Mam'zelle Clemence and guess what... She told me the Silver Spires Star contest is going to take place in the theatre! And guess what else... She's actually asked me to be part of a little committee to help decorate the theatre so it looks really striking and wow-ish! I tell you, Mia, I'm so glad I've got to know Mam'zelle Clemence through fashion club, because she's totally full of good ideas. This Star contest is going to be the coolest thing ever!"

My heart started beating too fast again. It looked like we were right back to my latest least-favourite subject.

Georgie leaned back on one elbow and squinted into the sun to look at Katy. "I'm afraid we've got a problem with our own particular star," she said, flapping a hand in my direction. "Mia doesn't want to enter."

"Oh no!" said Katy, sounding genuinely disappointed. She turned to me with pleading eyes. "I was so looking forward to sorting out your outfit."

I drew my knees up and hugged them tightly, feeling tenser than ever. I really wanted my friends to stop trying to persuade me to enter now, but I couldn't bring myself to talk about how much I hated performing in front of an audience and how it had built up over the years into this massive fear. So instead I decided it would be best to pretend it was all to do with the songwriting.

"This is turning into a nightmare!" I said, trying to sound a bit jokey and not show how upset I really was. "Apart from that one song you've heard, Georgie – which is far too babyish anyway – I've never written any lyrics, only music." I hesitated over the next bit, but decided to say it in the end. "And anyway, I'm just not the…performing type."

Georgie suddenly sat straight up again and put her hands up like a policeman stopping the traffic. "Hold it right there! I've had a magnabulous idea!"

We all laughed. Even me – though something told me I wasn't going to like this magnabulous idea.

"*You* might not be a performer, Mamma Mia, but *yours truly* most definitely *is*! So how about *you* write the music and play the piano, and I'll write the lyrics and be the singer!" She jumped up and came to sit close beside me and gave me a hug that was a bit awkward, because I was still clasping my arms tightly round my knees, trying to protect myself from all Georgie's wild enthusiasm. I felt like if I allowed myself to relax even for a second, I might be letting myself in for the dreaded contest. "I mean that wouldn't be breaking the rules, would it?" Georgie went on. "Miss York clearly said that you can have duets or even whole bands, as long as someone in the group has actually written the song, didn't she?"

I could feel that the others were all looking at me, waiting to hear what I'd say to this latest idea. And the truth was that I just didn't know what to say.

But deep inside my mind there was the smallest chink of maybe-that-would-be-all-right – maybe I *could* perform – beginning to show. I'd always dreamed of being a proper musician playing in front of a proper audience, and this could be my chance to prove myself if I just had the courage.

"Ha! She's thinking about it, I can tell!" Georgie announced triumphantly, grinning round at the others.

"Well, why not just do the audition and see how you get on," said Naomi. "Miss York said that it would only be herself and that new young music teacher, Mr. Ray, and Mrs. Harrison and Mam'zelle Clemence at the auditions, so it's not like having a whole audience or anything."

The chink was opening up. I liked Miss York, although I didn't know her all that well, as she's the Director of Music at Silver Spires and only teaches the seniors. She auditioned me before I came here though, because Mum and Dad entered me for a music scholarship – I was so happy when I heard that I'd got it! I didn't really know Mr. Ray either. He was one of those music teachers who just comes into school to teach individual pupils, like my own piano teacher, Mrs. Roach. Mrs. Harrison is our class music teacher, who's really nice, and I also like Mam'zelle Clemence, our French teacher, very much. Maybe I'd be able to manage it, as long as Georgie was there with me, taking all the limelight, and I could just play the piano. That would be all right. No one would really notice me. But then I found a new worry.

"My song's really quiet and slow. I just can't imagine you'd want to sing it, Georgie. It's not kind of...*whammy* enough for you."

Georgie smiled and looked round slowly and dramatically, then spoke in scarcely more than a whisper. "I can do quiet and slow, you know."

Grace giggled. "Oh, Mia, say you'll do it! You and Georgie would be such a popular act, I just know it!"

"At least play us the song after lunch, yeah?" said Katy.

The chink was starting to close up again. "I'll try it out with Georgie first..."

"Okay!" said Georgie. "That's a start!"

"But I'm not making any promises," I quickly added. "We'll just see if it sounds rubbish..."

Georgie gave me another hug then. "Oh ye of zippo confidence!"

* * *

After lunch we all trooped over to Hazeldean, because there'd be fewer people around there than in the music block.

"We'll wait in the common room," Jess said. "Come and get us when you're ready for us to hear it, yeah?"

So Georgie and I went into the little practice room and I started to play straight away so I could get it over with. I don't usually mind singing in front of Georgie, but even though she'd heard the song before I still felt a bit embarrassed singing it now. It suddenly seemed more babyish than ever singing about leaving people I love, and I'd hardly sung the first line before I stopped and dragged my hands off the keys, flopping them into my lap. "It's stupid, Georgie. I can't do it."

She sighed. "It is so not stupid, Mia! It's lovely, and I bet everyone else will sing loud in-your-face stuff."

"Exactly, because that's what's popular!"

Miss York had told us that anyone from Years Seven, Eight and Nine who wanted to be in the contest had to audition in front of the little panel of teachers first. Then, if they got through that all right, they'd sing in the first round of the contest, and there would be three rounds altogether, with people being eliminated each time. I cringed as I imagined me and Georgie managing the audition and then going on to sing in the first round of the contest. "What if we auditioned okay but then got no votes at all when there was an audience?" I said, feeling myself getting into a state.

Georgie pursed her lips and wrinkled her nose. "I don't think everyone will be told how many votes people get. It'll be like *X Factor* – they'll just say who's got the least, and those people will be knocked out." She tapped the piano impatiently. "Anyway, come on, finish it off."

But I didn't feel like it any more. Just playing the first line had made me realize more than ever how much the song wouldn't be suitable for Georgie's bouncy, bright character. And as I was thinking that, my fingers suddenly itched to find the right notes for that little phrase, *bouncy and bright*. The words were buzzing inside me and I put my hands on the keys and started playing their rhythm in the key of D major, which felt right. *Bouncy and bright, bouncy and bright...*

"What's that?" said Georgie urgently, staring intently at my hands. "What's that music you're playing? Did you make it up?"

Make it up... Make it up...

I didn't answer her straight away because I wanted to carry on playing now there were more words singing inside me.

"That's so cool, Mia! But just tell me, *did* you make it up?"

I nodded. "I've been doing it more and more lately. I get words in my head and I want to turn them into music, and then...I play them..."

Georgie squidged up beside me on the piano stool. "That means you're a natural composer, Mia!"

"No I'm not. I've only actually composed that 'goodbye' song."

"But all those bits of tunes are important too. They're like mini compositions. Honestly, Mia, I think you should turn them into a proper song. Then, hey presto, we've got ourselves an act!"

My stomach did a big yo-yo as a picture of Georgie and me on the stage of the wonderful big Silver Spires theatre came into my head. What if I felt sick again? I swallowed.

"Please say yes," said Georgie, turning to me with praying hands. "Pretty pretty please please *please*!"

And then it was happening again. My fingers were on the keyboard. *Pretty pretty please please please... pretty pretty please please please,* they played.

Georgie threw back her head and laughed. "You're a genius! I'm going to tell the others!" Then she rushed out of the room, but popped her head back round the door a moment later. "Carry on composing as long as you want. It doesn't matter about little details like afternoon school! I'll see you later when you've got it all ready!"

"No, Georgie, it doesn't happen as quickly as that..." I started to say, but I was talking to myself because by then she was probably at least halfway down the corridor.

Of course I didn't miss any lessons, because I'd never dare do anything like that. I've always been the kind of girl who obeys rules and does as she's told. I suppose it's just the way I've been brought up. But in the short time I had before the bell went for the start of afternoon school, I managed to work out quite a bit of melody and some words with a strong rhythm. It was in the kind of style that I knew would suit Georgie's voice, and I had to admit, I was quite looking forward to playing it to her.

She and I aren't always in the same sets for lessons, and on Wednesday afternoons we don't get to see each other till supper because apart from not having the same teachers, Georgie has drama club after school and I usually do my piano practice for Mrs. Roach at that time. But today for the first time ever I just couldn't concentrate on the work Mrs. Roach had set me because I was itching to get on with my song. I couldn't help it. I played it over and over, working out really good chords to go with the melody, and feeling myself getting more and more excited the more I played it. And as I kept practising, it was as if something within me began to change – like a tiny little spark of determination starting to grow and grow – until I realized that I'd made a decision. I was actually going to enter the contest. It would be terrifying, but I was trying not to think about that. In my heart, I knew I had to overcome my big block about performing in front of an audience if I wanted to be a true musician. I wanted that so much, and having Georgie on the stage to take the attention away from me seemed like the perfect answer.

At six fifteen she came into the practice room where I was playing away and I hardly glanced at her, just launched straight into my song. "See if you think it's all right, Georgie."

I rattled through the whole of it and at the end Georgie said, "Mia, you've gobsmacked me! Play it again!"

So I did, but halfway through I suddenly thought of loads of much better words, so I grabbed my piano-practice notebook from my music case and started frantically scribbling, while Georgie peered over my shoulder. It was just a big jumble of words on the page, but I knew I'd be able to sort it out and turn it into a proper set of lyrics, and as soon as I'd finished I turned to Georgie with shining eyes.

"There! I've done it – I've written a song for the contest! You convinced me I could enter, and I will. In fact..." I couldn't help giggling as I grabbed Georgie's hands. "...although I can't exactly say I'm looking forward to it, there's a teeny little bit of me that thinks it *might* not be too terrible!"

"That's great!" said Georgie.

But there was something wrong. Her eyes were darting about all over the place and she was biting her lip.

"What...what's the matter, Georgie? Didn't you like the song? You must tell me if you didn't like it... Honestly...I won't mind..."

But I knew I would mind really. I couldn't swallow properly thinking that thought, and I felt my mouth going all dry.

Georgie slid her fingers out of mine and looked down. "I think the song is totally fantastic, Mia.

21

Only…you'll have to do it on your own, I'm afraid, because I can't do it after all."

I stared at her and tried to speak, but although my mouth formed the shape of the word, no sound came out.

What?

Chapter Two

I tried again. "What? Whatever's happened, Georgie? What do you mean you can't do it after all?"

"Because of the Year Seven play," she blurted out. Then she gabbled the next bit really quickly, so I couldn't interrupt I suppose. "You know drama is totally my number one thing, and I know it's not a big-deal play like the one just before Christmas, but I've still got one of the main parts and loads of lines to learn, and the drama teacher says there's a rule that if you're acting in the play you can't take on any other commitments otherwise your schoolwork might suffer. So you see, I've got no choice. I can't not do the play, can I?"

She was willing me with her eyes to understand, and of course I did understand, but it didn't stop a huge disappointment weighing down on me.

"It's okay," I managed to mumble. Then I pulled myself together and tried hard not to sound so sulky. It wasn't Georgie's fault after all. I shouldn't have been relying on her to help me over my performing block. "It doesn't matter about the contest. I never would have even thought of entering it if you hadn't suggested it."

"Hey, hang on!" she said, opening her eyes wide. "I've just heard what you can do, and I honestly never realized you were so fantastic. I mean, I knew you could compose songs and everything, because of that other one you wrote – which I still think is lovely, by the way – but now I've heard this amazing new one I'm absolutely not letting you pull out of the contest. No way! You've got to enter on your own. You'll be miles better than anyone else, I bet you!"

I felt very flattered by what Georgie said, but I knew it wasn't true. "No I won't, Georgie. And anyway, I'm not doing it." I shook my head firmly, feeling my heart beat faster at the very thought of being on the stage on my own.

"Why not?" she asked, tipping her head to one side and planting her hands firmly on her hips, just as Jess, Katy and Naomi came into the room.

"How's it going?" asked Naomi. But then she noticed the way Georgie was standing. "Oh...what's the matter?"

So then Georgie had to explain about why she couldn't enter the contest after all. Her voice went soft and sorrowful as she talked, then suddenly seemed to snap to attention as she said, "But honestly, you should hear the song that Mia's just written. It's A-MAY-ZING. So I'm telling her she's got to enter without me, only she won't listen!"

"Will you sing it to us?" Jess asked me.

"It's not properly finished," I said. "I mean, I'm still fiddling with the words."

"But play them the music, Mia!" Georgie insisted.

So I did, and when I'd finished everyone said such lovely things I felt really sad that I didn't have the confidence to enter the contest myself.

"It's a Georgie song," I said a bit weakly. "I couldn't possibly sing it."

"Give me one good reason why not," said Georgie, looking exasperated.

"I'll give you five," I said, sticking my chin in the

air and striking them off on my fingers in the hope that this might be the end of the whole subject. "One, I'm not a performer; two, I'm not a singer; three, everyone else will be wearing make-up and I *never* wear make-up; four, I don't have any trendy clothes; and five, I'd just die."

But even as I was saying all those things, there was the faintest, most distant little voice deep inside my brain saying, *Are you sure you couldn't just give it a try, Mia? Then you can say you really are a proper musician.*

"So, that's a 'no' then," said Katy, which made the others laugh.

All except Georgie, who heaved a big sigh. "I feel as though I'm really letting you down, Mia," she said.

"No, you're not, honestly," I quickly reassured her.

"But there's another thing, too," she added. "My voice might be loud and vaguely in tune, but it's not good enough for the music you've written."

"Oh, Georgie, that's not true... Look, let's forget it now..."

"Well I don't know about anyone else round here, but I'm ready for supper," said Naomi, and for the second time that day I shot her a grateful look.

I woke up the next day feeling a bit upset. I'd dreamed that I was playing my new song on a big stage in London, and Kylie Minogue was singing it, but then I'd suddenly leaped off the piano stool, grabbed the microphone from her and taken over the singing in a really loud voice, while throwing myself round the stage doing crazy dancing, until I'd slowly realized that the audience was jeering at me and booing and starting to throw things onto the stage, and I'd kind of come to my senses and rushed off crying.

I knew exactly why the dream had taken place on a stage in London, because when Miss York had made her announcement in assembly all about the Star contest, she'd said there was going to be a big concert in London in the summer holidays to show off the singing and songwriting talent of British youth. It was open only to students under the age of fifteen and the winner of our contest was going to get the chance to audition for it.

During the morning, memories of the dream kept on seeping into my thoughts, which was horrible when I was trying to concentrate on lessons. But by the time school was over for the day, the dream had completely faded away, thank goodness, and while Georgie went outside to sunbathe and learn her lines, I went to do my piano practice.

I played a few scales to warm my fingers up, then opened my music book and turned to page thirty-six. The piece I'm learning for my piano teacher is called *Andante* and it's by Mozart. I put my hands on the keys and was about to start playing, when it suddenly hit me that it was a really boring title for a piece of music. *Andante* is Italian for *at a walking pace*. I began to play, but I felt as though my hands were plodding along, *plod plod*, and I just couldn't make the music come off the page into my fingers and out into the room.

So then I let my fingers skate off into their own music, and not just skate, but jump and skip and gallop. Only that felt wrong too, and in the end I snatched my hands off the keyboard completely and heaved a massive sigh. I needed to play something that felt completely right for that moment, and I knew exactly what that was. Georgie had bought me a book of *Mamma Mia* songs for Christmas. She jokes that that's her favourite show because of it having the same name as her best friend.

I reached into my music case for the book and opened it to the first song. As I played it, I was surprised to find it felt much more real to me than Mozart did. So I carried on to the next one, and the next, telling myself that time spent learning new pieces was good for me. After all, Mrs. Roach often says it's important to play lots of different music to help improve sight-reading. But in my heart I knew she wasn't going to be very impressed when I had my lesson the next day, because I'd not practised my set piece anywhere near as much as I usually did this week.

Eventually I came to a song that always makes me feel sad, and before I knew it, my eyes had wandered away from the music and started playing their own sad, slow melody. Then, note by note, it turned into the first song I wrote, my "goodbye" song. I didn't sing along to begin with, because I didn't feel like it, but after a while I couldn't help myself. The song wasn't complete without the words.

"You *see*!"

I jumped a mile at the sound of the voice right behind me. It was Georgie. I hadn't even noticed her coming in.

"You nearly gave me a heart attack, Georgie! I see *what*?"

"You see, this is a *Mia* song!"

"What do you mean?"

"You said that the last song you made up was a Georgie song. Well I'm telling you, this one's a Mia song. You've got to enter the contest with it, Mia. You sound brilliant singing it. I've hardly learned any lines because I've just been working out how to get you to realize that you've *so* got to enter! At least do the audition. Just that."

I don't know if it was because Georgie had called it a Mia song, or because the song felt so right that I'd actually lost myself in it, but something suddenly clicked in my brain, and I looked up.

"Okay, I *will* enter," I said simply.

And then I watched the expression on Georgie's face as it turned from surprise to shock to disbelief to...

"Yessssssss!" she squealed, as we both laughed and hugged each other.

Chapter Three

"Don't forget to take a deep breath before you start," said Georgie.

"And sit up tall and straight to give yourself confidence," added Naomi.

"And remember, you *are* good," said Grace. "It's such a cool song. You should be really proud of it! I've got to go to tennis now, but I can't wait to hear how you get on. Bye!"

As Grace rushed off, Katy pulled a strand of my hair round to the front, and smiled right into my eyes. "You look fab with your hair like that," she said. "Honestly."

I tried to smile back but my lips felt too dry.

"Pretend the teachers are all naked," said Jess. "That's what I was once told when I was really nervous about having to say a poem in front of an audience at primary school."

The others laughed and agreed that it was a great idea, and normally I would have found what Jess said really funny, but at that moment I was just too tense. It was exactly a week since I'd made my decision to enter the contest, and I'd done loads of work on my "goodbye" song, keeping to the same theme but changing most of the lyrics, and just playing it through over and over again so there was no way I could possibly forget any of the words or music, no matter how nervous I was.

We were all clustered together outside the drama hall, waiting for my turn to go in and face the audition panel of teachers, and I felt more scared than I'd ever felt before a piano exam. It turned out that Miss York wasn't on the panel after all, just Mrs. Harrison, Mr. Ray and Mam'zelle Clemence. I'd felt the teensiest bit less nervous when I'd heard that, but only for a second – then I'd started shaking again.

"Look it'll all be over in about three minutes," said Georgie. "So—"

She didn't finish the sentence because at that moment the door to the drama hall opened and out came a really pretty girl from Year Eight. She was wearing tight jeans with trainers and a white top, and carrying a guitar. She had amazing blonde hair, which fell in tumbly waves to her shoulders. I'd seen her around school but I'd never spoken to her before and I didn't know anything about her, not even her name.

"Good luck," she said to Georgie, breaking into a big grin. "It's a walk in the park, by the way, so don't be nervous."

"I'm not the one..." Georgie began.

"Oh sorry..." The girl's eyes flew round the rest of us, then she let out a little chuckle. "So which one of you is the lamb going to slaughter then?"

I gulped.

"It's Mia!" said Katy firmly, touching my arm to show who Mia was.

At that moment I wanted to run away as fast as I could, because I felt like a silly little girl next to this confident older girl. It's true that I'm the smallest in my group of friends, so I always look the youngest, but until this moment it had never mattered to me before.

The girl smiled. "Well, good luck, anyway."

"Er...do they...tell you if you've passed the audition straight away, or...?"

"Yeah, they'll tell you straight away. I think they're passing everyone as long as they're not complete rubbish, because not as many people signed up for it as they expected, apparently."

My legs trembled even more at those words, and the moment the girl had gone I turned to Georgie. "I've changed my mind. I can't do it. What if I'm complete rubbish and I'm the only one not to go through. Everyone'll know!"

"Don't be silly, you'll be—"

"Okay, Mia?"

Mrs. Harrison had popped her head out of the door and was smiling round at the five of us. I felt totally minuscule as I croaked, "Yes."

She pushed the heavy door open wide, keeping her hand on it to stop it closing. "After you, Mia." And I felt about six as I walked under her outstretched arm into the hall.

"Good luck!" said Georgie and the others, as Mrs. Harrison followed me in.

"Don't be nervous," added Naomi in a whisper.

I didn't turn round but Mrs. Harrison must have heard Naomi's words just before the door clicked shut behind us. "No, there's no need at all to be nervous, dear."

"Hello, Mia," said Mam'zelle Clemence, smiling at me from where she was sitting behind a table with Mr. Ray.

He glanced up at me and said "Hello, there," but his eyes went straight back to the paper in front of him, which had lots of writing on it. He wrote a few words at the bottom of the page, then turned it over and looked up properly as Mrs. Harrison sat down beside him.

"What are you going to sing, Mia?" asked Mam'zelle Clemence.

I tried to say, "It's called 'Time to Say Goodbye'," but only the word "Goodbye" came out, so I cleared my throat and said it again, and this time my voice worked, though it was shaky and my mouth was drier than ever. I walked on trembly legs to the piano, wondering how on earth I was going to be able to sing in this state.

"Just two seconds," said Mam'zelle Clemence, getting up to go over to the water dispenser in the corner. She pressed the little lever and out came the water, then she clicked over to the piano on her high heels and I smelled her lovely perfume as she handed me the beaker. "Take your time, Mia," she said in her strong accent. "Zere is nossing to worry about I promise you. Eef you go wrong, you start again!"

"It's not TV. You've only got the three of us watching you," added Mr. Ray, grinning.

Mrs. Harrison gave me a thoughtful look. "'Time to Say Goodbye'... That's a lovely title. What inspired you to write the song?"

"Er...it was when I was coming here to Silver Spires and I knew I'd be leaving my family."

She nodded and looked sympathetic. "Yes, I remember how sad I was to leave my parents on my first day at boarding school."

And as soon as she said that I got a picture of Mum and Dad waving to me as they drove off on that first day. It seemed a long time ago now. I'd stood beside Miss Carol, the housemistress, trying not to cry. I think Mum was trying not to cry too, because her smile was too bright.

I put my hands on the keys then and started to play, holding in my mind the picture of Mum and Dad's car disappearing down the drive, and after the opening eight bars of music I took a deep breath and started to sing, but I could hear that my voice was far too quiet. I told myself to keep going, because at least the words were coming out, which was something, and also I was managing to play without making many slips. But I was cross with myself. I knew I could play it ten times better than this, and when I'd played the last note I really wanted to ask if I could do it again, only I didn't get the chance.

"Thank you, Mia! That's a beautiful song," said Mrs. Harrison.

Mam'zelle Clemence said, "Well done, Mia," and Mr. Ray nodded briskly and smiled. But I thought they were just being kind and I felt a bit embarrassed.

"I usually sing it...better than that..."

"Yes, it's never as easy with an audience..." Mrs. Harrison leaned forwards and put on a grave tone. "Talking of which, how are you going to feel about singing and playing in the theatre with a big audience?"

I gulped as the awful memory of those two disastrous music festivals filled my head. I wasn't sure how I could answer that question. Were the teachers still trying to decide whether I was good enough to go through to the first round of the contest?

Mrs. Harrison was talking again. "Don't get me wrong, you sang it beautifully and it's a lovely composition, so we'd all love you to enter..." She looked at the others with raised eyebrows as if to check that they agreed with what she'd just said.

"Yes, eet was so beautiful!" said Mam'zelle Clemence.

Mr. Ray turned his palms up as if there was no need to add anything more but he would anyway. "Absolutely! Great!"

"We just want to be sure that you're completely comfortable about going onstage," said Mrs. Harrison.

I don't know if it was the compliments they'd given me, or just the fact that I'd actually survived the audition without anything too terrible happening, but my whole body suddenly felt more alive. I knew I had to push myself if I wanted to be a proper, performing musician, so I stood up quickly from the piano stool. "I know I was a bit quiet...but...I think I'll be okay."

Mam'zelle Clemence clapped her hands. "Excellent! Then we'll see you on Saturday for the first round...eef not before!"

Mrs. Harrison smiled at me as she walked me to the door. "Well done, Mia!"

And then I was in the corridor and a Year Nine girl, who everyone knows got a music scholarship to the school for playing three different instruments as well as singing, was walking in, while Mrs. Harrison stood against the door to hold it back for her. "Come in, Eve."

"So how did it go?" said Georgie.

"Tell us all about it," said Naomi.

Then Georgie again: "Did she tell you whether you'd got in?"

I nodded. "Yes, I'm in!" And the others jumped up and down, shrieking with excitement.

"Tell us all about it then," repeated Naomi.

So I did. And as we walked back to Hazeldean, my mind started to flit ahead to Saturday and I shivered with nervousness. "I must be mad! You saw how bad I was before the audition. What am I going to be like with a bigger audience?"

"Just be yourself," said Georgie.

"Don't do anything different from today," said Katy.

"Did they tell you how many acts are going to be competing?" Jess asked.

I shook my head, and I think that was the moment when my spirits plummeted and a big cloud of depression came over me, because I pictured the Year Eight girl with her lovely tumbling hair and her guitar, and then I recalled Eve strolling into the hall as though she didn't have a care in the world. I bet

Mam'zelle Clemence didn't have to get any water for *those* two. They were natural performers.

"Do you know the name of that girl who auditioned before me?" I asked my friends glumly.

"Bella," said Katy. "She's in fashion club. She's got some amazing clothes."

I sighed and stopped walking abruptly. "I feel so young and boring," I said miserably. "It's one thing doing the audition, but I'll look pathetic onstage next to beautiful Bella and talented Eve."

"Look, Eve plays in orchestras and bands and things, doesn't she?" said Georgie. "That doesn't mean she's any good at singing, does it?"

"She sings in choir and she's got a beautiful voice," I said with another big sigh. "And what about Bella? She'll be in all her trendy clothes and I'll look like a pathetic little girl."

"No you won't," said Katy. "Because I'll make sure you don't! Have faith, Mia. I'm going to make you look stunning! Clothes, hair, jewellery, make-up, the lot!"

Georgie nodded firmly. "Never fear, your mates are here!"

And I had to smile then, even though it was a bit wobbly.

Chapter Four

I couldn't see the look on Mrs. Roach's face because she was sitting, as she always does during my piano lesson, to the side of me and on a slightly lower stool, and anyway I was staring at my music and concentrating with all my might. I knew I should have been playing this piece so much better than I was, and I couldn't help feeling a bit ashamed of myself.

Because I was awarded a music scholarship to Silver Spires, I get a big reduction on the school fees. But one thing that Mum and Dad were told was that it was really unusual to award a music scholarship to a student who only played one instrument and hadn't had singing lessons. I felt so thrilled when I heard about my scholarship, and Mum told me it was because I was on grade six at the time, and had great potential, but she said the music department at Silver Spires were hoping I'd take up another instrument, like the flute or something, so I could play in the school orchestra. Every so often Mrs. Harrison asks me if I've got any plans to take up a second instrument and she's even said she's going to talk to my parents about it, because I really ought to join the orchestra in Year Eight.

"Just keep going," said Mrs. Roach a bit impatiently, and I felt my cheeks going pink. I was playing *Andante* terribly, and the more I played, the more it showed up that I hadn't done anywhere near enough practice. Eventually, when Mrs. Roach still wasn't saying anything, I dragged my hands off the keys and looked at her.

"Sorry, it's not very good, is it?"

She pursed her lips and gave a small shake of her head, with a disappointed look on her face.

"I've...I've been doing lots of sight-reading though."

Why wasn't I just telling her straight out that I hadn't been practising my piece because I'd been putting all my energies into improving the song I'd written for the Star contest, and also playing pop songs and songs from musicals?

"Well I'm pleased to hear that you've been sight-reading but you can't afford to just leave your set pieces and scales, Mia. They're the things that strengthen your technique and deepen your general musicianship, you know."

I nodded.

"Is it that you don't particularly like the Mozart? I can easily start you off on a new piece."

Mrs. Roach is quite a kind lady. I think she must have been teaching piano for years because she's fairly old, and I often wonder what it must be like to be stuck inside a little room all day long, with pupil after pupil stumbling through their pieces. She only comes to Silver Spires two days a week, but I think she goes to other schools on the other days. The piano teacher I had before I came here often used to set me jazz pieces and occasionally even pop, but Mrs. Roach has only ever given me classical music to play and I think she's too set in her ways to change now. I'd certainly never dare suggest playing a *Mamma Mia* song in my lesson, or anything like that.

"Well, what about the Mozart? Shall we stick with it or start something new?"

"Er..." The little room felt suddenly too hot. "Can we start something new?"

She nodded and turned to the contents page of my book of classics. "There's this Beethoven, which is a lovely piece. Or what about this Debussy? I think this would suit you, Mia."

I wanted to ask her what she meant by that. What kind of music did Mrs. Roach think suited me, and how could she tell, when she didn't really know me at all? But it somehow seemed a bit of a bold question to ask. It's strange with one-to-one teachers, because they treat you differently from the way ordinary teachers treat you, and you feel as though you can say a bit more to them, but in the end they're still your teacher, so you can't completely relax. At least, you can't with Mrs. Roach.

There's a girl called Annie in Willowhaven House who learns the trumpet, and she says her teacher is totally cool. Annie can chat to her teacher about all sorts of things, like her hair, or the meals at Silver Spires, or worrying about not being able to do her prep. She told me the main reason she loves the trumpet is because of her lovely teacher.

I looked at Mrs. Roach and imagined myself asking her advice on how I should wear my hair on Saturday night. No, I could never do that in a million years. She'd probably just say I should tie it back, because that would be sensible, and basically she's a sensible person.

"Er, can you play the Debussy for me please, Mrs. Roach?"

She raised her eyebrows. "Well, I'll give you a few bars, yes."

So she did. And it was really beautiful, but seemed very difficult.

"Is it a bit hard for me?"

"No, dear, it'll stretch you a bit, but that's what we want, isn't it?"

I nodded, but there was something niggling away at the back of my mind, asking me if that was really what I wanted.

We always talk about a new piece of music for ages, Mrs. Roach and I, and I managed to answer all her questions about key and metre and expression and phrasing and dynamics, but I was only paying attention with half my mind, because the other half was trying to pluck up the courage to tell her about the Star contest. I just felt that she might be more understanding about my practice if I told her what I'd actually been doing and how I was beginning to love playing other kinds of music as well as classical. It was silly of me not to mention it, and in the end I made myself just get on with it.

"Er...there's a kind of music competition coming up on Saturday, Mrs. Roach, that I'm entering."

"Oh right, yes, I think Miss York might have mentioned some sort of contest to me...only I thought it was a pop song competition." Her whole face seemed to snap to attention. "Dear me, that doesn't give us any time at all to prepare. I hadn't realized it was an actual music competition." Mrs. Roach was getting herself into a real state. Her nostrils were doing the little flaring thing they do when she's in a stress because one of her pupils is late. "What is it, a general instrumental competition, or just for pianists?"

"It's...a...singer/songwriter contest."

Her face relaxed a bit. "Oh, so not a proper music competition? Just for fun?"

Why did that make me feel suddenly annoyed? "No, it *is* a proper competition. It's called the Silver Spires Star contest and it's a bit like *The X Factor*..."

"Oh, I see. Phew! I thought we'd missed a real chance to show off your piano skills!"

It was really making me mad that Mrs. Roach wasn't interested in a single word I said – she only cared about her precious classical piano. I should have gone with my feelings and kept quiet, but now I'd started I had to carry on.

"I've written a song and I'm accompanying myself on the piano."

"Lovely! Well done you! So…does that explain the lack of practice?" She was looking at me with a mixture of a smile and a bit of a telling-off. I wished she'd realize that I'm not nine.

I spoke in my most mature voice, but I could feel my cheeks burning hot. "I've been working on my composition quite a bit because…" I raised my voice slightly to emphasize what a big thing the contest is. "…the winner gets to audition for a huge national event in London."

She broke into a beam. "Well, that is exciting. And the contest is on Saturday night, you say?"

I nodded and wondered whether at long last she was taking a proper interest.

"All right, so I won't expect much practice from you until that's over then!"

"It's only the first round on Saturday night. The people who are voted through have to compose and perform a different song for the final round a week later, and that's in two parts. So, say there were eight people, then it might go down to four at first, then there'll be another vote to find the winner."

"Right…" Mrs. Roach's eyes had moved off my face and were back on the Debussy, and I could tell she wasn't really interested. "Okay, let's have a bash at this. Try to hear the first couple of bars in your head before you start."

But the only thing I could hear in my head were angry thoughts about Mrs. Roach and I don't know how I managed to get through the rest of my piano lesson without exploding. It was obvious she thought the Star competition was a trivial little nothingy contest, and what made me even madder was the way she was also assuming that I wouldn't get through the first round, because she never said a word about how my practice might suffer if I was busy writing another song.

It was all I could do not to slam the door when I went out of the music room. I didn't look at Mrs. Roach when I said goodbye, and I stayed angry all the way from the music block back to Hazeldean and up to our dorm, which is on the top floor. There was no one in the dorm and I threw myself face down on my bed and burst into frustrated tears.

After a while I turned over and stared at the ceiling. I should never have mentioned the competition to Mrs. Roach because I know she doesn't get pop music. But what made it ten times worse was that she was probably right not to worry about me missing any more practice, because there was no way I was going to get through the first round. In fact, it was a stupid idea entering this contest. I'm not a performer so I'm never going to be a real musician.

"Hey, Mia, what's the matter?" Katy had come back from fashion club and was clambering up the ladder to my bed. She stepped over me and squashed herself into a corner, leaning against the wall and hugging her knees. "I was only just thinking about you actually."

I wasn't sure whether to answer her question or to ask her why she was thinking about me.

"We've been at the theatre," she went on excitedly. "We're going to make loads of huge Ss out of thick silver paper – but not that shiny sort of stuff – a real brushed-metal look. And we're going to hang them all over the theatre in chains. That was my idea!"

"It sounds brilliant!" I said with as much enthusiasm as I could, but then Georgie came crashing in, back from her play rehearsal.

"The Star list is up outside the drama hall!" she announced dramatically. "Eleven acts, including quite a few bands." She was climbing the ladder to my bed as she spoke. "Shove up, Katy!" Then she looked at my face properly for the first time and her voice went all soft and worried. "Have you been crying, Mia?"

I didn't answer, because for some reason my throat was hurting and I could feel tears starting to prick the backs of my eyes again.

"Oh Mamma Mia, what's the matter?"

I sat up and hugged my knees, so we were all three sitting side by side, our backs against the wall. Part of me was tempted to admit how petrified I was at the thought of performing, but I just couldn't.

"Mrs. Roach made me mad, that's all."

"Mrs. Roach? Was she cross because you hadn't practised enough? Did you tell her you've got to... you know...what's that word? Begins with P?"

Naomi came in then. "Wow, Mia's bed! Definitely the 'in' place, I see!"

"What's that word, Naomi? For when you sort things out in order of importance, you know, you have to pri..."

"Prioritize."

"That's the one. I hope you told her straight, Mia!"

So then I was annoyed with myself because Georgie was right. I was just too meek and mild. I should have been stronger with Mrs. Roach.

"She wouldn't have listened," I answered in a flat

voice. "She didn't think the contest was anything important. As soon as I said it was a singer/songwriter competition she lost interest."

"Oh poor you, Mia! Well, listen, that's Mrs. Roach's problem. Just ignore the old bag."

Georgie always sticks up for me brilliantly, and that's what she was doing right now, and yet, even though I was cross with Mrs. Roach, I didn't want anyone calling her an old bag. It was all a bit confusing. I do like Mrs. Roach, and I respect her too, but she'd just got to me that afternoon.

Naomi looked thoughtful. "You should try to get her to come along to the first round on Saturday night. Then she'd see how talented you are at writing your own music."

I shivered at the thought of Saturday night. My heart beat at five hundred miles per hour every time I imagined the auditorium at the theatre filled with people all there to watch eleven acts...including me. I wasn't sure if the Year Tens and Elevens would be interested in a contest for the younger girls, but if they were, then there might be about three hundred and fifty people there, and every one of them would be voting for one of the acts. My heart raced even more and I wondered how I'd ever get myself onstage on Saturday evening.

I thought about what Naomi had said. It was a lovely compliment, but I wasn't sure if I wanted Mrs. Roach to be at the contest. It would only make me more nervous than ever.

"Anyway, forget about that," said Katy. "The important thing is, what's Mia going to wear?" Her eyes gleamed and she sat up straight. "That's what I want to know!"

As soon as Grace was back from tennis and had got changed, and Jess was back from doing her art project, we all sat round on the rug in the middle of the lovely old oak floorboards of our dorm. We'd only got about five minutes before supper, but Katy thought we ought to have a friendship meeting to get everyone's opinion on what I should wear on Saturday night.

"We've got to consider the whole look," she said, narrowing her eyes in thought. "Not just the clothes, the image."

"Well I think we need to make you look older, Mia," said Georgie, nodding round at everyone as though they were sure to agree.

"But we mustn't make her look too different from what she is," said Naomi.

"Wh...what *am* I?" I asked in a small voice.

"You're natural," said Naomi simply.

"Yes, Naomi's right," Georgie said with a sigh. "You're little and slim, with long straight blonde hair and lovely creamy skin, and I'm deadly jealous. Why can't I have long straight hair and be all small and neat?"

"Your hair's lovely," I said, "and at least you look your age!"

"What do you *want* to wear?" asked Jess.

"Just jeans and a top."

"Well, we'll let you wear jeans," Katy said thoughtfully. "But I think we need to snazz up the top half. What about this?" She jumped up and went over to her drawer. "Hang on a sec..."

She came back with a beautiful bright turquoise top with swirly patterns of sequins all over it.

"But that's one of your best tops, Katy! And it might be a bit big for me..." Although even as I was saying it, I was really hoping it would fit, because I so wanted to wear it.

"It'll look great with your blonde hair," said Katy. "Go on, try it on."

So I did, and I absolutely loved it.

"It looks way better on you than it ever does on

me!" said Katy, which was very kind of her but totally not true.

So then we all went off to supper talking about what make-up I ought to wear. After supper we had to get through an hour's prep, which is like homework, where we sit in a room in silence and get on with the work we've been set. Tonight it was our matron, Miss Jennings, supervising. I couldn't concentrate particularly well, and I noticed Katy wasn't concentrating either. She was sketching away with a dreamy look in her eyes, while, on my other side, Georgie had her play script on her lap. I glanced sideways at her and saw her lips moving, which meant she was learning her lines.

The moment prep was over we rushed back up to the dorm so Katy could try out some make-up ideas. When she'd finished, I looked at myself in the mirror and got a shock at the sight of my face with bright red lips and silvery black eyes. I thought I looked like a horrible doll, but I didn't want to say that when Katy had worked so hard.

"Do you think you need to soften it a bit?" Naomi asked carefully.

"I'd really rather not wear any make-up at all," I said, trying to be a bit less meek and mild.

Naomi and Grace agreed that if I wasn't

comfortable in make-up, I shouldn't wear any, but Georgie and Jess said that I'd look pale and washed out on the stage with all the bright lights if I didn't wear some sort of make-up.

After I'd washed my face, Katy had another go, and I liked it much better, because although it gave me a shock when I looked in the mirror, it wasn't a nasty one. Really, it was still a bit too much for my liking, but I knew Georgie and Jess were right about the stage lighting, and everyone said I looked stunning – even Naomi and Grace – which was a lovely compliment. So I agreed to let Katy make me up just like that on Saturday.

Saturday! I shuddered yet again and couldn't get the thought of it out of my head. By the time I went to bed I was in a terrible state, imagining all the cool acts coming onstage one after the other, and then pathetic little me wandering on, and people not really noticing me because I'm so small and young-looking. Or maybe I'd have to go on first? Would it be worse to be first, or last, or somewhere in the middle? I decided the middle would be best.

After a while I could feel that I was the only one still awake. I could hear Georgie, Jess and Naomi breathing, and although the other two sleep almost completely silently, I've been in the same dorm with them for so long that I can just tell when they're asleep. And as I lay there, feeling very alone, I started thinking about the piano, which got me into an even worse state.

Every single week since I've been at Silver Spires I've gone straight to a free practice room after my piano lesson and practised for a few minutes, because Mrs. Roach taught me that if you do that, all you've learned will stick in your memory, whereas if you leave it even for a day, you can't remember what you've been taught half so well.

Today, though, for the first time, I hadn't played through any of the work that Mrs. Roach had set me. I'd just kept playing my song for the contest, and then I'd spent ages improvising new bits of songs. It seemed to be all I wanted to do these days and I couldn't help feeling guilty about it. There was a horrible little voice at the back of my mind reminding me that I'd got my music scholarship because of my piano playing, and I shut my eyes and buried myself under the duvet to try and stop the terrible picture that came into my mind of a stern-looking Mrs. Roach telling me I hadn't practised enough.

You know what this means, don't you, Mia? You'll have to give up your scholarship.

I shot out from under my duvet, feeling stifled.

If I had my scholarship taken away I might have to leave Silver Spires, because I wasn't sure if Mum and Dad could afford to keep me here without the school paying some of my fees. And that would be unbearable.

I promise to practise like mad from now on, I told myself over and over again as I lay in the dark. *I promise to practise...I promise...*

Chapter Five

As Friday turned into Saturday, and Saturday morning turned into Saturday afternoon, I grew more and more nervous. The girls who were performing in the contest had to attend a rehearsal in the afternoon to check the position of the mikes and the sound levels. Mr. Ray was also going to tell us the running order. We had to be at the theatre between two o'clock and two thirty, and I decided to be early to get it over with more quickly. Georgie said she'd come with me, thank goodness.

I'd been worrying in case Georgie wasn't allowed to be with me, but when we turned up, Mr. Ray didn't tell her she had to go or anything. It was a relief to find I was the first to arrive.

"Now, let's see..." He pulled a sheet of paper out of his pocket. "You're the fifth act of eleven, Mia, so you'll be seated in the auditorium with your friends, and you'll come down to the stage when you're announced." I like the way the seats in the auditorium are in tiers, getting higher as they go further back, just like a proper theatre. And the front row is level with the front of the stage. "It's all very casual," Mr. Ray went on. "Nothing to worry about. If you want, you can give the audience a little wave or a bow, or otherwise you might prefer simply to go straight to the piano."

"I'll go straight to the piano," I said in a small voice.

"No probs at all!" said Mr. Ray. "Now, this is the mike for your voice. You can sing a bit now to get an idea of how close to the mike you need to be, and you'll notice that with the amplification on the stage the piano will come over nice and clearly."

I didn't feel nervous in front of Mr. Ray, because he'd heard me sing before, but I was just about to try a few bars of my song when I heard whispering and noticed that a group of Year Nines had come into the auditorium, two of them carrying guitars.

They were all chatting quietly.

Mr. Ray must have seen me looking anxiously up at them because his voice dropped. "Don't worry about them. The soundcheck is important, Mia, so that we get it right tonight. Also, it's good for you to get used to singing into a mike."

"Go on, Mia. Just sing the first bit," Georgie tried to encourage me. But I hesitated, because the Year Nines had all stopped chatting and were standing perfectly still waiting for me to begin, and that made a wave of nervousness come flooding over me.

Mr. Ray frowned. His eyes darted from the girls to me and back to the girls. "Sorry, you lot, would you mind waiting in the green room, please? I'll come along and get you in a few minutes. If you pass anyone else on your way, give them the same message, please."

The girls all exchanged eye-rolling glances, and my cheeks flooded with colour. I felt such an idiot needing the teacher to make the big girls go away before I would sing, and then I felt even worse because just before they went out I clearly heard one of them say, "Why's she bothering to enter if she can't even sing in front of us?"

"Just ignore them," said Mr. Ray. "It's easy to be confident when you don't have to get up onstage and perform solo. Those girls are all in a band. Now...let's see...is this mike angled right? Just sing the first bit of your song and I can adjust it..."

So I did, and it sounded strange to my ears.

"Well that's pretty much perfect." Mr. Ray smiled. "Let me quickly check from the back." He leaped off the stage and ran up the stairs, two at a time. "Okay, shoot!"

I felt a bit more confident this time and sang a few more bars than I had done before.

"Great!" Mr. Ray gave me a thumbs up and then leaped back down to the stage and asked me if I was happy.

"Not exactly," I said, pulling a face to show how nervous I was.

He laughed. "But apart from feeling nervous, happy with the stage?"

I nodded.

"Just one more thing to bear in mind. There will be a strong spotlight on you all the time, so you won't be able to see the audience at all."

I nodded and swallowed.

"Okay, that's fine. See you later then! Make your way to what we call the green room, just along from the auditorium, at about seven, then Miss York will give all you contestants a last-minute talk before sending you through to the auditorium to sit with your friends. Okay? You know where the green room is, don't you?"

I nodded. My parents knew someone who worked at The Royal Festival Hall in London and he had told me all about the green room there, where the performers gather before concerts. There are drinks machines and nice settees and tables, and places where you can hang things up. Then, when it's time for you to go onstage, it's easy to walk from there to the wings at the sides of the stage. I hadn't been in the green room at Silver Spires before, but I'd walked past it, so I knew where it was.

I couldn't eat any supper that evening, and by the time we were back in the dorm and I was all dressed up in my jeans and Katy's top, I felt sick.

"This is such a bad idea," I whispered shakily. "I never should have entered, should I? I'm just not the right person for this kind of thing."

As Katy did my make-up, the others tried to keep me calm.

"You don't know if you're that kind of person yet," said Naomi. "You love playing and singing your song, don't you?"

I nodded.

"So you're halfway there, right?"

I nodded more slowly. It didn't feel like halfway there. It felt like a hundredth of the way there.

"Stop talking!" wailed Katy. "I get lipstick all over her face every time she nods!"

Naomi ignored her. "Well, there you are, Mia. Once you start singing, you'll forget about the audience. And remember, with the spotlight on you, you won't be able to see them anyway, so you can pretend they're not there!"

I hadn't thought about that until Naomi said it, and it actually calmed me down...well, just a little bit.

Georgie grinned at me. She was crouching down in front of me, peering at my face as best she could whenever Katy's arms or hands weren't in the way. "Naomi's hit the nail on the head, as usual, Mamma Mia." Her grinning face suddenly appeared really close up. "And I have this hunch that you're going to find it's totally fab onstage! Because it *is*!"

I couldn't help smiling. Georgie always cheers me up. I'd still not breathed a word to anyone about my embarrassing experiences when I was little, because I couldn't even bear to think about them myself, let alone tell anyone else, yet it seemed at that moment as though Georgie could see right inside my head.

"Good, you're not twitching around so much now," said Katy. "I can finally get this done!"

I might not have been twitching on the outside, but my insides were like quivering jelly.

"Right, take a look!"

There's just one full-length mirror in the dorm and when I looked in it I couldn't believe that it could be me standing there, looking so tall in Katy's wedges and so sophisticated in her sparkly top. My hair looked strong and sharp too, instead of soft, because Katy had used her hair straighteners on it. But the biggest change in me was the make-up. It looked just right for the clothes I was wearing. I'd never seen my eyes sparkling so much.

"Thank you, Katy," I whispered.

She grinned. "Pleasure, madam!"

But I wasn't sure if I was comfortable with this new image. It felt like I was hiding the real me inside this sophisticated look and, in a way, as if I was cheating myself of being natural. Grace gave me a lovely smile in the mirror as she quietly said we ought to be going, and I knew she understood how strange I felt all dressed up like this when I'm not used to it, because Grace is exactly the same as me where fashion is concerned.

When we got to the theatre, the first thing that hit me was the noise. There were masses and masses of girls milling around in the foyer, and loads more who'd already gone to sit down in the auditorium. I spotted plenty of Year Tens and Elevens, and I gulped, because it meant it would be a massive audience. There were lots of teachers there too, all dressed up as though they were off out for the evening, which added to my anxiety, because it seemed as if they were treating the night as specially important. Music from the speakers filtered into every tiny chink of air space that wasn't already filled with chatter or laughter, and the strong smell of perfume made the air even heavier.

"What am I supposed to do? Where do I go?" I asked Georgie in a sudden panic.

She put both hands on my shoulders. "Calm down, Mamma Mia. You go to the green room, don't you? That's what Mr. Ray said."

Georgie was right. I was in such a state I couldn't remember the simplest thing.

"Look, there's Mam'zelle Clemence beckoning you over, Mia," said Naomi.

It was a relief to see Mam'zelle Clemence's smiling face across the foyer and I made my way over to her.

"We'll save you a seat in the auditorium," Georgie called after me. "See you in a sec."

I followed Mam'zelle Clemence into the green room and found it was almost as noisy as the foyer, even though there were only about twenty people in there. And everyone looked so glam, in skimpy figure-hugging dresses or tight trousers with the highest heels. Katy might have done a big transformation act on me, but I still felt like I was the least dressed-up person in the room, and I was suddenly grateful that my hair hung in a curtain. It would help me to hide my face from the audience.

Bella, the Year Eight girl who'd done her audition just before me, was standing in the middle of the room. There were several Year Eights and Nines crowded round her, all talking loudly as though there was a competition to find the loudest voice. Another girl was playing the piano in the far corner, and five or six people were tuning their guitars, though how they could hear a thing, I didn't know.

"Eef you want to play ze piano, Mia," said Mam'zelle Clemence above the noise, "I can ask Lily to give you a turn. She 'as been prrractising for ages."

"Er...that's okay."

Then she was gone to join Miss York and Mrs.

Harrison, who'd just come into the room. Miss York clapped her hands for silence and everyone was immediately totally still and quiet. And yet something *was* moving in the room. I could feel it. Maybe it was just the atmosphere, trembling with theatre magic.

"Well," she began, her eyes sparkling, "I don't think anyone was expecting quite such a huge audience! This clearly is the social event of the year!"

While some of the girls turned to each other and grinned, another Year Seven called Louise, who's in a different house from me, gave me a nice smile and mouthed, "Are you nervous?"

I nodded and she hunched her shoulders up tight like a little girl and mouthed, "Me too!"

Louise wasn't the only Year Seven girl in the room, I noticed as I glanced around, and I felt relieved about that, because I'd been too nervous to notice anything except the number of acts when I'd looked at the list.

"I know you're all going to be fantastic," Miss York was saying, "because I have it on very good authority that your auditions were wonderful!"

Mrs. Harrison nodded hard, which made some of the girls laugh.

"Okay, so eleven acts this evening. Now, just to reassure you, if you're playing in a band, the keyboard and drums are all set up and ready. For the girls playing piano rather than keyboard, the piano is ready too and the mike is in place if you're singing from the piano. I think Mr. Ray warned you all that the spotlight will be on *you* when you sing?" She put on a really dramatic voice as she said that, and there was the smallest rush of laughter that wavered and then shrank away, as though everyone had finally realized how scary it was going to be on the stage. I felt relieved that I wasn't the only one who was nervous, though I knew without a shadow of a doubt that I would be the most scared of all.

"How many acts are going through to the next round, Miss York?" asked Eve.

"Important question! I was just coming to that. We're going to reduce the number of acts from eleven to seven tonight."

We all nodded and exchanged nervous smiles.

"Now, don't worry, you won't be stuck in this room all evening. I want you to be able to see each other's acts and vote for them, so you'll be called down from the auditorium when it's your turn and then you can return to your seat when you've finished. So, all I have left to say is have fun and don't worry if you don't get through to the next round. You've all shown that you're fantastically talented, both for being able to perform your songs, and some of you for writing the songs in the first place! Okay, Chloe, you're first up, so the rest of you can go and join your friends now."

"Good luck, Chloe!" came all our voices, but Chloe looked as though she was in a world of her own, busy giving her guitar a last-minute tuning. How could she be so calm? I think I would have died if I'd had to go on first.

Chapter Six

My friends were about halfway back and it looked as though every single seat in the auditorium was taken, right to where the teachers were sitting in the back two rows.

"I've got your voting card," said Georgie, flashing a yellow card at me as I sat down beside her. "I'll look after it till you're done. Are you okay?"

"There are so many people here," I said shakily, instead of answering her question. "Year Tens and Elevens and all these teachers! Why is it so popular?"

Georgie rubbed her hands together as the lights

went down and the curtains swooshed open. "Because it's good fun!"

I gulped and stared at Miss York, who was standing in the middle of the stage. It was starting. This really was it.

"Welcome, everyone! What a magnificent turnout! And don't worry, I'm not the first act!"

Everyone laughed. Then Miss York went on to say how exciting the evening was bound to be, and told the audience to clap all the acts equally hard, "because it's nerve-racking performing a song in front of so many people, especially if it's the first time you've done anything like that". She then reminded everyone that each song had been entirely written either by the soloist or by a member of the band performing it, and pointed out that it was a very difficult thing to do, even for the most musical people. "I don't think I could do it, actually!" she added, which made the teachers laugh. "And I want to thank the music department for helping us nurture so much talent at Silver Spires." There was more clapping.

"So, let's get the show on the road, as they say, with the first of our eleven acts this evening. Ladies and gentleman, please welcome to the stage, Chloe Canning!"

Chloe came smiling on to the stage, holding her guitar by the neck as though she was strolling along to her next lesson. Then she put her free hand up, pretending to shield her eyes from the spotlight, which made a few people laugh. She looked completely relaxed as she sat on the high stool in front of the mike and started to play, but after only a few seconds she suddenly stopped and said, "Whoops! Forgot the title!" which caused another wave of laughter. "Okay...my song is called 'The Clouds Block the Sun'."

Chloe's song was a folky type of pop song, with verses and choruses and strummed guitar chords. She sang in a clear, strong voice and didn't forget a single word, even though it was a very long song. I really liked the lyrics. Each verse told of a different sad situation, then the chorus came back to the idea that the clouds were blocking the sun.

When she finished, the audience clapped and whooped loudly, then Miss York returned to the stage and my heart thudded with nervousness. Chloe bowed, then came up into the auditorium to find her friends. You could hear them all congratulating her as Miss York started to speak.

"Thank you, Chloe! It's tough being first to perform and you made a great job of it. So now let's have our second act…" Miss York peered into the auditorium. "I can't see a thing, but can I have Danni Maloney and Sarah Shore next, please!"

They were already approaching the stage and I knew them both, because they're Year Sevens, though not from Hazeldean. Danni went to the piano and Sarah to the mike at the front of the stage. Mr. Ray zipped onto the stage from the front row, where he was sitting with Mam'zelle Clemence, and moved the stool out of the way because Sarah wanted to stand.

"Our song was written by Danni," she said, "and it's called 'Stick Together'."

Sarah's voice was beautiful and she swayed as she sang, looking as though she was really getting into the music. I didn't know how she could do that with so many people watching her.

After Danni and Sarah, it was Eve's turn. She walked quite briskly to the piano and adjusted the stool as she sat down. My heart started to thump as I craned my neck to see whether she was lowering it or raising it. I knew it was a silly thing to be worrying about, but the stool had been exactly the right height for me in the afternoon, and I didn't want to have to adjust it before I played. It would just make me more nervous than ever with everyone watching. What if

I turned the handles the wrong way and had to do it again, and everyone was fed up with waiting for me? Mr. Ray would probably jump up and start helping, and those Year Nine girls from the band might start sniggering.

I'd got myself into such a state that my palms were sweating, so then I worried that my fingers might slide around on the keys and I'd play all the wrong notes and get booed off the stage. But next thing I knew everyone was clapping loudly, because Eve's song had finished. I'd been in such a panic, I'd hardly heard any of it. The audience seemed to love it though. Loads of girls were whistling and whooping while Eve stood there bowing.

Georgie squeezed my hand as the first band of the evening went down to the stage. "You're better than Eve!" she said, grinning. Then she asked Naomi if she'd got a tissue, and a few seconds later I got one passed along to me from Katy. "There you go, Mamma Mia. To wipe away those nerves!"

It was lovely that Georgie was looking after me so well and I wiped my hands hard.

The band Demonstrate consisted of five girls – one on keyboards, one on drums, two guitarists and a singer. All of them had got crazy, frizzed-up hair and wore body glitter and funky bright, tight clothes.

They looked amazing, and their song was so clever, with its different instruments blasting out loudly. Normally I would have loved it, but all I could do was shrink down into my seat and feel my throat getting tighter and tighter. There was no way I could sing after this. I'd sound ridiculous, like a little girl being allowed to recite a poem at a grown-ups' party, especially as these were the girls who Mr. Ray sent out of the theatre when I was about to sing at the rehearsal.

"You're just as good as Demonstrate, too," said Georgie.

I shivered. Now I knew for sure that she was only saying things to make me feel better, because there was no way I was anywhere near as good as the band. The main singer seemed to get more and more confident, throwing her voice out and really moving with the beat, just like a professional singer. Sometimes all five girls suddenly sang together, which was a brilliant effect, and as they got near the end of the song, it grew even louder and stronger and finally people started clapping in time with the music, until the crescendo hit one final note and the girl on drums whacked the cymbal with all her might.

As the applause rang round the auditorium my stomach turned over and over and all I wanted to do was run away, or hide under my seat.

"Wow, that certainly woke us up!" said Miss York, as the band left the stage. "We've tried to create a nice varied programme for you, though, so next we have Mia Roberts. Please welcome her to the stage!"

Georgie thrust a water bottle in front of me and said, "Drink!" I did as I was told, then all my friends whispered, "Good luck, Mia. Good luck!" and I stumbled on shaky legs down to the stage, wondering how I was ever going to get through the next three minutes.

"Just relax," came Mr. Ray's quiet voice from the front row as I passed him. I didn't think anyone else would have heard.

I sat on the piano stool and thought it was the right height, which was a relief so then I leaned forwards and spoke into the mike. "My song is called 'Time to Say Goodbye'."

There was a single whoop from the audience which I recognized as Georgie's, but it made everyone laugh and I felt pleased that there was a bit of noise to make a background for me to start playing while no one was quite ready. It seemed like only a microsecond later, though, that the theatre was completely silent apart from the piano and my voice. My hands weren't shaking, thank goodness, but I could hear a tremor in my voice, and all the time I was singing, my head was spinning with anxious thoughts. Was I loud enough? Was I playing too slowly? Would I remember the words? Was my song boring? Would Mrs. Roach have liked this song if she'd been here? Which teachers *were* here? What would happen when I finished? Would anyone clap? What if no one clapped?

Pictures of that long-ago audience laughing when I got the name of the composer wrong at the age of six, and of my eight-year-old self rushing from the stage to be sick, came flashing through my mind, but a moment later I felt as though the music of my song was carrying me away and all my other thoughts vanished.

As I sang the last note of all I held it for a little longer than usual, because I was dreading there being a silence after it. Eventually I had to let it go, though, and my hands dropped to my lap. For a second there was not a sound apart from my heart thudding, but then it felt as though someone had switched on a waterfall where the audience was sitting – that's the only way I can describe it. The noise of clapping just whooshed and roared and splattered, and the relief was one of the best feelings I've ever had.

Nothing mattered any more. I'd managed to play my song. I hadn't enjoyed it, but I'd done it and now I could go back to Georgie and relax for the rest of the evening. My legs were shaking so much I don't know how I made it to my seat but somehow I did and then Georgie was hugging me.

"You were amazing!" she said. "I'm so proud of you!" And the others all leaned over and tried to pat me.

"Well done!"

"Brilliant!"

"Right, let's turn up the volume again," Miss York was saying, "but not a lot, with a song from... Bella!"

There was something different about the way Miss York had announced Bella and I couldn't think what it was at first, but then I realized that she hadn't said her second name, which she had for the other soloists. I wondered if that had been Bella's idea. She walked thoughtfully and slowly down to the stage, holding her guitar by the neck, and halfway down the stairs she looked back at her friends, who all cheered her loudly. She swung back round to carry on walking and her hair swung too, like in an advert. When she got onto the stage, she strolled to the stool and sat down carefully. She was wearing the most amazing short, tight, black dress, and round her neck she'd wrapped very thin strands of glittering silver beads.

"She looks great!" I heard Katy whisper to Naomi. And I agreed, Bella looked really beautiful.

When she announced her song title, I noticed that she'd got shiny gloss on her lips. "My song is called 'Is Anyone There?'"

Whoops sprang like fireworks from all over the audience, and then Bella began. It was easily the best song of the evening. It was somehow stronger than my song and a little faster, and Bella sang the words with such passion that the audience's silence seemed to grow even deeper. I couldn't take my eyes off her and I never wanted the song to end. It was reminding me of home, sitting round on Sundays with a proper fire blazing, and Dad saying, "I *do* like a fire!" and grinning at me and Mum and Robby. And outside the wind would be restlessly scooping and billowing, but in our living room we were so cosy. By the time Bella finished, I had tears in my eyes. Her music really had made me think I was at home, and I suddenly longed to talk to Mum and Dad. As soon as the show finished, I'd go off on my own for a little while and call them.

The clapping continued long after Bella had

bowed and left the stage, and it was obvious she was the most popular act so far. No wonder. She was beautiful *and* talented. Even though I knew I wouldn't get through to the next round, I made a promise to myself to compose more songs, because Bella had truly inspired me.

There were five more acts that followed, but none of their songs had the same magic as Bella's. Of the five, I probably liked the two bands best, especially the one called Twins Plus One, who really did consist of twins plus one. Their composition was very simple and straightforward, but it was also lively and bright and that seemed to be what the audience wanted. I knew for sure now that there was definitely no way I'd be voted through with my quiet little song.

The other band, who were from Year Eight, was called The Craze, and I didn't think they were as good as Twins Plus One. Then there were two girls who sang solo and accompanied themselves on guitar. And the last act of the evening was a duet. Two girls from Year Nine sang a cappella, which means without any accompaniment at all. They called themselves Contemporary Counterpoint and they kept the audience absolutely spellbound, which I thought showed what talent they'd got, because you'd think the audience might have got a bit bored after ten other acts.

"I liked them," said Naomi simply, when they'd finished.

Georgie wrinkled her nose. "Not as good as that... what's her name?"

"Bella?" I offered.

"No... Oh, what's her name...? Oh yeah, Mia Roberts."

"No, nowhere near as good as her!" said Naomi and Katy together.

I laughed, but I knew it wasn't true.

At the end of the last act, Miss York asked the audience to get ready to cast their votes on the yellow cards. All of us performers had to go up on the stage while Miss York reminded everyone of our song titles. We each had to take a step forward when she said our name, and I noticed some of the contestants waved or did big over-the-top bows. I just smiled a bit shakily. The audience clapped and stamped and whooped and whistled. Then, as pens for the votes were passed along the rows, we were allowed offstage to go back to our places. Georgie handed me back my card and I wrote *Bella* on it when a pen came round to me. "I don't mind if you vote for Bella," I said quietly to Georgie.

She looked at me as though I'd just said I didn't mind if she voted for the man in the moon. "Don't be ridiculous, Mia!"

Then all my friends held up their cards to show me that they'd written my name down and I wondered whether I might only get their five votes out of the whole audience. Thank goodness we wouldn't ever know how many votes each act got.

Five or six teachers, including the four organizing the evening, collected up the cards, and then some pop music came pounding and surging round the auditorium while the teachers went off to count the votes. About twenty minutes later the music faded, along with the loud chatter and laughter, and Miss York was back in the centre of the stage. I once read the phrase *a breathless hush*, and for some reason or other those words popped into my mind at this moment. There was not even a murmur as Miss York began to speak.

"Well, what a tremendous evening this has turned out to be. I'd like to start by thanking Mam'zelle Clemence, Mrs. Harrison and Mr. Ray, for dreaming up the idea in the first place and for organizing it so wonderfully. Thank you." There was loud clapping, but it didn't last very long and it was obvious everyone wanted to get on to hearing the votes.

My heart was hammering again as I wondered if all the contestants would have to stand at the front, tensely waiting to see whether they were going to be voted off. What if Miss York decided to do that?

Georgie gripped my hand again, and I saw that she was gripping Katy's on the other side. In fact all my friends were holding hands tightly, as though that might somehow magically stop me being voted out. But it wouldn't, of course, and even though I'd already told them a million times there was no way I'd get enough votes to go through to the next round, they still seemed to be hanging onto the hope that I might.

"Now, I'm *not* going to ask our performers to come onto the stage, because I think that's a bit cruel to be honest. I'm simply going to announce in a random order the seven acts with the greatest number of votes, who'll be going through to the next round." Miss York paused and smiled round, as I swallowed. "So, here we go!"

My heart started banging away again, which made me get cross with myself. There was no point in hoping for a miracle. I must just relax and be happy that I'd done my best and survived a terrible ordeal, and that I can go back to concentrating on my work for Mrs. Roach and writing songs for fun.

"The first act to go through is..." I could have counted up to about ten in the pause. "...Demonstrate!"

The audience roared and the girls from the band, who were sitting across the aisle from me, all jumped up and started waving their arms in the air.

"Next to go through..." The pause was just as long as the last one. "Twins Plus One!" Another massive cheer.

"Third up, we have...another band...The Craze!"

From out of the audience like a rocket came a long drawn-out "Yesssss!"

"Fourth of our seven finalists is..." I was used to the long pauses by now, and in my mind I was saying the name Bella, so I got the shock of my life when Miss York said, "Mia Roberts!" My heart turned over with happiness, and Georgie and the others all stood up and cheered as though they were the stars of the whole night, but I didn't care. I don't think I've ever felt such a surge of joy in my life as I felt at that moment.

"And fifth tonight...Bella!" This time the roof really was raised, and I just knew Bella must have got the most votes. I turned round to see the two friends on either side of her patting her on the back and hugging and kissing her, while she sat quietly in the middle. In my head I added another point to the list of *Amazing Things About Bella*. She's also modest.

"Number six of our acts to go through…is… Contemporary Counterpoint!"

"And lastly…" This pause must have gone on for twenty seconds and I felt so sorry for the remaining contestants because only one of them was going to feel fantastic, while the other four were probably going to feel rubbish. "…Eve Proctor!"

The audience, that had been holding its breath for so long, let it out in a massive sigh that seemed to me to be scattered with broken dreams, while the little knot of people around Eve exploded out of their seats with cheers and air punches. Then everyone was getting up and rushing around congratulating people. I stood in the aisle surrounded by Georgie and the others, who were all telling me how brilliant I was.

It was a truly magic moment, full of lovely thoughts about breaking the wonderful news to Mum and Dad, and of writing more songs and working and working to get better so I'd get through the next round as well, and… Then I realized with a shock what I'd just been thinking. I was actually looking forward to being onstage and performing in front of an audience. It was as though there was a bright light shining inside me, full of a kind of determination and ambition that I'd never felt before. And in that moment I knew for sure that I'd finally overcome my terrible block about performing. I could even call myself a real musician at last. And the relief of knowing that, was better than a thousand Christmases and birthdays all rolled into one.

Chapter Seven

"Hi, Mum, it's me!"

"Hi, you! You certainly sound excited! And no wonder! Dad and I were so excited when we got your text last night. It's brilliant that you got through, Mia! Come on, tell me more about the contest. I want every detail!"

"I'm so happy!" I squeaked. Then I tried to calm down a bit so Mum could actually hear what I was saying. "Well, there were seven of us out of eleven who got through. And I've got to write another song in only a week, but I've already written quite a lot of it, and it's a bit more upbeat than the last one, and I know I'll be nervous all over again, but not half so much as last time because I think I've finally got over my big block about performing in public."

"Oh, Mia, that's wonderful, love. You must have had to be so brave, but well done for managing it. We're so proud of you."

I smiled and smiled on my end of the phone.

"And if you get through the second round will you have to write another song?"

"No, because the final round takes place on the same evening, only it's in the second half, and you can sing either one of your two songs. But there's no way I'll get through to the final," I quickly added.

Then Mum wanted to know what the various bands and soloists had sung and I told her in big detail about the other acts in the contest, and how the winner will go through to the auditions for the big concert in London, which Miss York has told us is called *Stars in the Wings*. "It's so exciting, Mum, because you can only audition for *Stars in the Wings* through your school and Miss York says that the schools will only put forward their very best talent."

Mum said she thought that sounded wonderful, then she came back to what I'd said about having to write another song in such a short time. "I know you said you'd done lots already, but...is there much still left to do? I'm just a bit anxious that it's taking time away from your proper practice."

There was that irritating word again – *proper* – the word Mrs. Roach had used in my piano lesson. I couldn't help snapping this time. "It *is* proper practice when I'm composing and trying out my own songs."

There was a pause and I knew exactly what was coming next. "Yes, but you won't let the work you have to do for Mrs. Roach suffer, Mia, will you?"

I snapped again. I couldn't help it. "Well it might suffer a bit, but it's only for one more week."

"And if you won the contest, would you have to write something else for the London show?"

I hadn't been expecting Mum to consider that question in a million years, and I stopped being annoyed with her immediately because I felt so pleased that she even thought I stood a chance of winning the contest.

"Oh, Mum, I'd absolutely love to win, but there's no way I could ever do that. I mean, I probably only just scraped a place in the second round. The bands were fantastic, and it's a really high standard all round, but the very best act is a solo singer from Year Eight. She's called Bella and it's obvious she's going to win the whole thing. Everyone's saying it."

Mum tried to soften her voice a bit. "You will make sure you explain to Mrs. Roach that you'll practise properly as soon as the competition is over, won't you? It's great that you've managed to perform but I'm sure I don't need to tell you, darling, the school made it very clear that your scholarship really does depend on you excelling in your piano lessons."

I didn't say anything, but I could feel my hackles rising, and I wasn't exactly sure why.

"You see, the thing is," she went on, "you can't show your talent in any other way, as you don't play an orchestral instrument..."

And then I got it. That's what was making me mad. Not only was writing songs not "proper" music, but apparently it didn't show any talent. All the effort I put into creating words and music and arranging them together into something that people enjoyed enough to vote for didn't count for anything in Mum's and Mrs. Roach's eyes.

"I know," I mumbled, thinking how often I'd had that fact drilled into me.

"And you know that without the help with the fees that we get from the scholarship, we wouldn't be able to afford to...to keep you at Silver Spires?"

I swallowed and nodded, then realized Mum

couldn't hear me nod. "Yes, I know that too," I said a bit snappily.

I hated sounding all stressy like this but I couldn't help it. I probably should have just told Mum why I was cross, but I didn't have the energy, so we talked for a few more minutes about my friends, and how my schoolwork was, and how my little brother had come first in a fancy-dress competition, and how Mum was going on a jewellery-making course the next weekend. And then we rang off and I folded my arms and sighed noisily.

"What's up?" came Georgie's bright voice. She was walking towards me from Hazeldean. It was Sunday afternoon and we were just chilling. She knew where to find me because whenever I phone home, I always walk up and down the main Silver Spires drive as I'm talking, unless it's raining.

"Mum's been reminding me about my music scholarship," I told Georgie glumly.

"What about it?"

"You know...how important it is that I've got to keep making progress on piano so I don't lose my scholarship."

"But you *are* making progress. Playing all sorts of different pop stuff and jazzy stuff and musicals and things. You never used to take any interest in those kinds of things before. You should tell her, Mia, that you're – what's the expression? – broadening your horizons. That's what you're doing!" She beamed at me. "I'm quite proud of that actually!"

"You're proud of me broadening my horizons?" I felt really touched. "Hey, thanks, Georgie."

"No – well, yes, I *am* proud of you doing that, but I mean I'm proud of myself for thinking of the expression."

I couldn't help laughing. But I was also grateful to Georgie. She'd come up with such a good phrase and I would make sure I used it next time I spoke to Mum. I might even dare to say it to Mrs. Roach.

"I just talked to my mum and dad too," Georgie carried on brightly. "They said it was a horrible day and they were sitting around indoors doing nothing much. Isn't it amazing how the weather can be so different a hundred kilometres away? I mean it's hot and gorgeous here. I'm going to change into a short skirt. See you round the back, yeah?"

She rushed off and I was left there full of thoughts. Something Georgie had said had shot me straight back to thinking about Bella's beautiful song. What was it?

I walked back down the drive towards the gate, and found myself humming a bit of it. It was amazing that I'd remembered it so well. And immediately I thought about Mum and Dad and me and my little brother sitting round the fire. Yes, that's why I'd been reminded of Bella's song in the first place. Georgie was talking about her mum and dad sitting around doing nothing much because of the weather being bad, and I'd imagined them in their living room with some music on in the background, because that's what *my* family used to do at home on gloomy days. And even when Bella had been singing in the theatre the evening before, I'd been taken right back to those cosy times around the fire at home.

But why? Why had Bella's song made me think of that? It was weird. I hummed the tune again, but this time I managed to carry on to the next part too. And then I stopped walking and stared at the ground. Some words were coming into my head. *You paint a golden circle round your dreams to keep them safe inside...* But those weren't the words that Bella had sung, were they? No, I was sure she hadn't sung anything about golden circles and dreams. And yet, in my head, those were the words that went with that tune.

I started walking again and something clicked so sharply that I froze. The reason I was singing those different words to Bella's music was because I'd heard them before. I'd heard Bella's melody but with those words on one of Dad's CDs that we used to sometimes have on in the background when we were sitting round together on rainy days. So...was it just a coincidence? Or...or did Bella write new words to an old song?

The hairs on my arms stood on end. If she did, then...she cheated, because the one and only rule of the contest, the rule that stopped so many people from entering who might have entered otherwise, was that you had to write whatever you sang yourself. Could Bella have cheated? No, it was a ridiculous thought. She wouldn't have dared. The rule was so strict and clear that *no one* would have dared. I must have made a mistake. I must have. I wasn't going to think about that stupid song on Dad's CD any more. It was obviously nothing more than a big coincidence that her song had sounded a bit the same in places. I mean there are only so many notes to play around with, and only so many different rhythms, so it's not surprising that sometimes music comes out sounding similar to other music.

All the same, I felt like someone sleepwalking as I set off to meet Georgie on the lawn at the back of the main building, and as I got nearer, instead of going round the side of the main building I found myself going off in the other direction, towards the music block. I wanted to be on my own a bit longer, and, more than that, I wanted to sit at a piano and just play. It might calm me down.

I couldn't get my worry out of my head and I was searching my brain to try and remember more about the song from Dad's CD. His collection of CDs is so enormous and full of different music and artists that nobody's ever heard of. Mum always laughs when the subject of Dad's CDs comes up. "Your dad's taste is totally and utterly individual," she says. "I think there must be a category in the music shops called *WEIRD* where he goes to buy his music!"

I stopped walking and made a decision. I would phone Dad and ask him what the song was called. What did Bella say the title was? "Is Anyone There?" Yes, that was it. Usually Mum hands the phone to Dad after she and I have been talking together, but this time we both forgot, probably because we'd wound each other up about my scholarship.

My heart raced as I listened to the ringtone.

"Oh hi, Dad."

"Hello, Mee." Dad's always called me Mee for as long as I can remember. "Glad you phoned back. Thought I must have done something wrong when Mum rang off without passing you over."

"Sorry, Dad. I don't know why we both forgot. Mum said you got my text about me getting through to the next round of the Star contest."

"Yes, we certainly did! I was just about to text you actually, but you know what I'm like with texting. Takes me half an hour to write two words! Yes, well done for the contest. What a star!"

I laughed, then swallowed and took a quick breath. "Dad, I was just trying to remember a song on one of your CDs."

"Oh good! I'm glad someone appreciates my taste in music."

"I can't remember who the singer is, but I think the song's called 'Is Anyone There?'"

"'Is Anyone There?'" he repeated slowly, and I could practically hear his brain ticking over. "Hang on, I'll have a look. Not so many to look through now, though. I went a bit mad clearing out when we had the living room redecorated, and I took quite a few CDs down to the Oxfam shop... Let's see... Tell you what, I'll ring you back. It'll be quicker if I've got both hands free."

My heart was beating really quickly and I felt all tense and anxious while I was waiting for Dad to phone back. What if he found the song? What would I do? Who would I tell? I couldn't find any answers because the questions were too big.

In the little practice room I started playing my own song, the more upbeat one I'd started to write when I thought it was going to be me and Georgie singing together. I'd spent ages working on it earlier in the day, changing loads of the words. I'd called it "My Best Friend and Me". Georgie had come tiptoeing into the practice room after about an hour to bring me a hot chocolate, and she'd dramatically whispered, "Don't speak, Mamma Mia," as she'd put it on the cupboard by the piano. "Don't even say thank you. It'll break your concentration!"

Good old Georgie.

I'd changed the style of the original song to make it slower and gentler than before, but it was still more upbeat than "Time to Say Goodbye" and although I knew the speedier tempo would probably add to my nervousness when I came to perform it, I definitely wanted it like that. I just didn't seem to be able to stop giving myself new challenges.

There was a lot more left to do with the song though. I had to improve the arrangement until I felt completely happy with it, and then sing it over and over until I could do it in my sleep, because that was the only way I'd be confident enough to perform it the next Saturday. Thinking about that now made a big twang of nervousness ping through me, but it vibrated with excitement too and I knew it was a good kind of nervousness.

I was so into singing the song that I completely forgot about Dad phoning, so it gave me a massive jump when my phone suddenly started to ring.

"Hi, Dad." My heart was racing again.

"Hiya, Mee. No luck, I'm afraid. Can't find that title anywhere. Can you give me any other clues? Was it a solo artist or a band or what?"

I frowned as something struck me. Maybe "Is Anyone There?" wasn't the real title. If Bella had changed the words to the song, she might have changed the title too.

"Not Gordon Lightfoot, the folk singer?" Dad was saying.

"I really don't know, Dad."

"What do you want to know for anyway?"

"Oh...I just heard something which sounded really similar, and it reminded me of when we used to sit round the fire on rainy weekends."

Dad didn't say anything and I knew he'd be imagining the scene I was painting.

"Shall I...sing you a bit, Dad?"

"Go on then."

So I sang the bit I remembered as best I could,

but it wasn't very much to go on.

"Yes, I *think* I know which one you mean...I'm not a hundred per cent, mind... What's his name? Oh...I'd forget my head if I didn't have it screwed on... Yes...is it Jed Jarrow? That's the only one that springs to mind. I chucked that CD out, Mee, I'm afraid."

"It's okay, don't worry, Dad. I was just wondering... that was all."

"Mum says you're making up another song this week." Dad changed the subject a bit.

I didn't want to get back to talking about scholarships, so I pretended somebody had come into the music room and I had to go.

I'd hardly disconnected when there was a tap at the door and I looked up at the small window in the top of the door and saw Bella's smiling face, which gave me such a shock. Immediately my cheeks went pink. She couldn't possibly have heard what I'd been saying, because the rooms are soundproofed, but I still felt guilty.

She mouthed, "Okay to come in?" and I nodded and tried to smile.

"Spotted you through the window," she began, then she let a giggle out. "Thought I'd come and say congrats and all that!"

"Oh thanks! S-same to you!"

"Thanks!" She giggled again and leaned her elbow on the top of the piano, propping her chin on her hand. "It was exciting, wasn't it? I'd never have guessed there were going to be that many people there! And everyone was so supportive, the way they clapped and cheered and made us all feel good about ourselves."

Bella sounded really friendly and warm. It was nice of her to come and talk to me, but I knew I wasn't acting naturally, because all the time she was talking I was trying not to stare at her, and half wishing I dared to ask her where she'd got the idea for her song from, or something like that. But I didn't have the courage. My voice would have come out all croaky or I'd have gone bright red.

"I was so nervous," I managed to say quietly, biting my lip.

"Me too. Terrified!"

I tried to act a bit more normally. "You'd never have guessed. You looked completely calm!"

She giggled again. "I was like a duck actually, all smooth and serene on the surface, but underneath, paddling like mad!"

I laughed. It was such a good way of describing how you somehow manage to keep terrible nervousness inside. "Have you...started your next song yet, Bella?"

"Yes, I'd already got the idea for another song ages ago so I was crossing my fingers like mad that I'd get through. What about you?"

I nodded and immediately felt uncomfortable again, because my mind just wouldn't seem to let go of the idea that maybe Bella cheated.

"Oh well, I'd better be going. See you on Saturday!" She put on a sort of *yikes* face and we both laughed nervously. Then she was gone, and I was left with my horrible thoughts.

But I shook them away as hard as I could. They were winding me up too much. Bella was lovely. It didn't make any sense. She'd never cheat.

Would she?

Chapter Eight

"Don't forget what I told you," Georgie said for the millionth time. "You've been *prioritizing*, right?"

I nodded and sucked my lips in to stop them feeling so dry. Georgie and I were walking past the tennis courts. She was about to go to a play rehearsal and I was going to my piano lesson, feeling more nervous than I'd ever felt before about one. Until just recently I'd always been bursting to show Mrs. Roach how much work I've done. Not today though.

The lesson always starts with scales and I usually rattle up and down them, feeling my fingers loosening up ready for my set pieces. But today I was dreading playing scales, even though I had actually done them quite a lot to keep my hands supple for playing my song. The reason I was dreading them was because my heart would be sinking more and more with each one, waiting for the awful moment when I had to play my Debussy. And I didn't know what on earth Mrs. Roach would have to say about that, as I'd only practised it for about an hour in the whole week, instead of my usual four hours, and if I was honest, I hadn't enjoyed it particularly because I so wanted to work on my song.

Maybe I'd be able to distract Mrs. Roach. Wouldn't it be great if it turned out that she was really pleased with me, and wanted to listen to my composition for Saturday. Then we could waste loads of time talking about the Star contest.

"Come in, Mia," she beamed, when I knocked. "Gemma Wright was away so I've had a gap. Pity you couldn't have taken her lesson as well as your own! I'm so looking forward to hearing how you got on with the Debussy."

I groaned inside and my lovely *talking-about-the-Star-contest* castle in the air came tumbling to the ground. This was going to be a terrible piano lesson, just as I'd thought. Maybe I ought to pretend I'd been ill. Yes, that would be best. Otherwise I had the feeling that Mrs. Roach would be really cross.

"Right, let's start with those scales," she went on brightly, as I unpacked my bag and sat down.

There was a tap on the door and Mr. Wagstaffe popped his head in. I think he teaches sax. He's another young teacher, like Mr. Ray, and he's got long hair and wears his shirt hanging out. I noticed Mrs. Roach frowning at him, then raising her eyebrows, but she didn't say anything.

"Sorry to disturb you, Mrs. Roach. Do you have a spare pencil by any chance? Or a sharpener? You'd think there'd be a few knocking about somewhere in a music department this size wouldn't you, but—"

He had to break off his bright chatter because Mrs. Roach was holding out a pencil that she'd whipped out of her bag in about two seconds flat. Mr. Wagstaffe looked a bit taken aback and I felt sorry for him. He'd only asked for a pencil, after all. I gulped. If a teacher interrupting her to borrow a pencil could make her as impatient as this, goodness knew what was going to happen when it turned out that her scholarship pupil had hardly practised all week, for the second time in a row. Well, at least not the kind of practice that she approved of.

As soon as Mr. Wagstaffe had gone, Mrs. Roach

spoke through tight lips. "Right, let's get down to business. E flat melodic minor."

I played it without a single mistake and felt pleased that everything was all right so far.

"Good. And sticking to that key, E flat minor in contrary motion."

I managed that one without any mistakes too.

"Good, you've really got the pattern into your fingers now. Just a little more emphasis on the accents and don't lose speed at the outsides. Try it again."

We spent about five minutes on scales and Mrs. Roach taught me a new arpeggio pattern too.

"Well done, Mia. You've picked that up beautifully!"

I smiled shakily and hoped that my good scales and arpeggios might count against the bad stuff that was coming next.

"Okay, let's get down to the Debussy!" She rubbed her hands and looked really excited. "If I know you, you've thrown yourself into it, right?"

I swallowed. "Er, actually, I've not been very well this week, Mrs. Roach, so…"

"Oh dear! What's been the matter?" She was looking carefully into my eyes and I felt myself going a bit pink because it felt as though she could tell I was lying.

"Well...I've had a cold, only it was quite bad. I've not really had the energy to practise more than my scales..."

She frowned. "Really? Oh dear! Didn't you have that pop song competition at the weekend? Did you have to drop out?"

"Er, well, I didn't get my cold till Sunday, luckily!" I smiled nervously at her, but she didn't smile back.

"You seem all right now."

"Yes, well, nearly."

Mrs. Roach didn't look convinced and I felt my mouth going dry with worry, but when she spoke again she sounded softer and I felt relieved that it looked as though she was letting me off this once. "Oh dear, so how much time *have* you put into the Debussy?"

"Not really very much. I can play the first page..."

She nodded and tried to smile, but I could tell she was still a bit annoyed. I'd never told a lie to Mrs. Roach before, and I felt guilty and ashamed for having to tell one now. But then I felt cross again, because it wasn't fair that she didn't think music was important unless it was classical. I looked at her with her bright eyes, and heard Georgie's voice in my mind.

Tell the truth, Mia. Say you've got to prioritize. Make her realize that you're broadening your horizons.

But somehow, I couldn't.

I just about got through the first page of the Debussy but I wasn't very proud of the way I played it, and when I'd finished Mrs. Roach was clearly disappointed.

"You *have* been under the weather, haven't you!" was her first comment. There was a pause after that, then she must have decided not to waste another single second. "Right, let's get to work. First of all, pedal. I know you haven't learned the notes, but there's no excuse for poor pedalling..."

"You said *what*?"

Georgie was pretending to be cross with me, but actually she might have been genuinely disappointed.

"I said I'd been ill. It was just...easier, Georgie."

"Hmm," was all Georgie said. But then she gave me a hug. "Sometimes I despair of you, Mia Roberts."

I grinned, because I could tell she was enjoying acting the part of a fond mother.

"Sometimes, I despair of *myself*!" I told her

truthfully. "I'm getting all nervous about Saturday again now. I was wondering what I can wear for a start. I don't have any clothes that'll look right, and I can't wear Katy's top again."

"We'll ask Katy," said Georgie, flapping her hand as though that was nothing. "Now come on, let's get over to the dining room. I'm starving."

The build-up to the final rounds of the competition was just as bad as for the first round, and by the time Saturday evening came I felt sick again. The only thing that helped was remembering that after tonight the whole thing would be over. The seven remaining acts were to be voted down to three in the first half, and then after the interval, the overall winner would be decided on.

"You look stunning," said Naomi, her head tipped to one side as she looked at me. "You really do."

"Yes, you do," Grace agreed, smiling at me and nodding to show she really meant it.

"You ought to play your song to the others, Mia," said Georgie. "I know I keep going on about it, but it'll get a bit of nervousness out of you."

"Yes, please play it for us, Mia," said Jess.

The six of us were in the dorm, getting ready for the show. All my friends were so excited. They'd spent ages changing into their coolest clothes and doing their hair, just as though we were all going out to a posh restaurant or something. And all over Silver Spires there was a buzz in the air. Everywhere you went you could hear people talking about the Star contest, and making bets about who would get through.

"Go on, Mia," said Katy and Naomi at the same time.

"Georgie's right," Naomi added. "You'll feel more confident once you've tried it out in front of a mini audience."

In the end they persuaded me to sing it for them, so we all trooped off to a practice room. My friends stood behind me, apart from Georgie, who stood at the side, and when I finished playing and singing I realized with a shock that I'd actually forgotten they were in the room with me. I really had lost myself in the song.

Katy was the first one to speak. "Oh wow, Mia. You're really amazing, you know! Your voice is so much stronger than last week." Then every one of them gave me compliments.

"You see, I was right, wasn't I?" said Georgie,

doing her fond-mother act again. "I bet you're not so nervous now, are you?"

I grinned at her and had to admit I felt much better. But as soon as we started walking over to the theatre, the butterflies were back in their swarms. And by the time we were inside the theatre building, the swarms were swirling madly.

"It looks as though everyone's got here early to get the best seats," said Georgie, glancing into the auditorium. "We might not even manage to sit together this time."

It was such a little thing, but it scared me ridiculously. I wanted my friends to be in a group so that I could imagine them when I went onstage, even though I knew I wouldn't be able to see them because of the lights.

When I pushed the door to the green room open I felt as though all my energy had left me. I was suddenly faced with loads of cool, super-trendy outfits and I just felt like a little girl again. Katy and Jess had promised me I looked nice up in the dorm in front of the mirror, and I'd even dared to think it myself. The two of them had covered one of my plain tops with sequins and bits of glittery material. It was so kind of them, because it had taken ages, but they'd insisted on doing it themselves, and kept on making jokes about how professional performers weren't allowed to sink so low as to do their own costumes. I was wearing a pair of plain black trousers on my bottom half, with a pair of Katy's black shoes. My outfit was finished off with a beautiful, wide, black and white belt, also Katy's.

"Hiya, Mia!" came a bright voice as I hovered by the door. It was someone from the Year Nine band, Demonstrate. None of the girls from that band had said anything to me when I was in the green room last time, and I think they'd probably still despised me then because of Mr. Ray sending them out of the theatre when I'd been practising in the afternoon. But now that I'd got through that first round, I must have earned their respect, and that brought a bit more confidence back to me.

"All right, Mia?" said Bella, catching my eye from across the room. She beckoned me over to her and my stomach muscles tightened instantly as my mind flashed straight to my dad and his music and my fear that she'd cheated.

"Hi. Here we go again!" I was trying to sound laid-back, but I knew my voice was a bit shaky.

"What are you singing tonight, Bella?" asked one of the twins from Twins Plus One, her eyes big and round.

"Oh, just something I've called 'Fairy-Tale Ending'," said Bella, looking down.

"Wow! I bet it's amazing," said the other twin. "Where do you get your inspiration from? I mean, how do you actually go about writing your songs? Because we managed the first one okay, but we're not sure if our second one is any good."

I was glad she'd asked that question, and my heart started racing as I wondered how Bella would answer. She looked up at the ceiling for ages and then shrugged slowly and turned her palms over as though it was a mystery. "I guess it just comes," she finally said softly. "I suppose I kind of fiddle about and wait for it to happen, you know!"

By this time quite a few more people had formed a little group around Bella, but she didn't look at anyone as she talked, so she didn't seem like she was showing off. "It doesn't always work. Sometimes I feel my creativity is blocked and I know there's not even any point in trying to compose at those times. But, then at other times, it just kind of pours out of me!"

You paint a golden circle round your dreams to keep them safe inside…

I closed my eyes for a second to try to make those words go away. I didn't want to hear them, now of all times. I needed to concentrate on my own song at the moment. And anyway, there was still a chance I'd been mistaken. I listened to the twins praising Bella, and I looked at her outfit. Tonight she looked even more fantastic than the last time. You couldn't help staring at her, because she was so stunning. She'd twisted her hair in a knot on the top of her head and pushed a silver slide into it, which seemed to be all that was keeping it in place. Her dress was made of green velvet that swirled out at the bottom, and her shoes were dark green and very pointy. I just knew that Katy would love the whole outfit.

"Ooh, beautiful dress, Bella!" said Miss York, coming over at that moment. "Is everyone happy over here? Yes?" She smiled round at us all. "All warmed up?"

I nodded and the others said they were as warmed up as they'd ever be, and things like that, so Miss York stood on a chair and clapped her hands for quiet.

"Well, here we are again, girls!" she began, which made a few people chuckle. "Now, the order of events for this evening is – listen carefully – Eve first, then The Craze, followed by Mia, then Twins Plus One, Bella, Contemporary Counterpoint and finally, Demonstrate." Miss York threw a special smile out to us all. "And then there'll be the voting to eliminate four of those acts." I glanced at Bella and she must have sensed my eyes on her because she immediately flashed a smile in my direction. "After a short interval," went on Miss York, "we'll move to the second part of the evening, in which the three remaining acts will sing again."

"But we weren't supposed to prepare another song, were we?" asked one of the Demonstrate girls, her eyes filling with panic.

"No, no," Miss York reassured her. "If you get through to the final round you can either sing the same song again *or*, if you prefer, you can sing your song from the first round. And then finally a winner will be found!"

The girls from the bands immediately turned to one another and started talking in whispers about which song they'd sing if they got through, while Eve, Bella and I just stood there. Eve and Bella looked as though they were concentrating hard, but the only thing I was concentrating on was flexing my fingers to warm them up. There was no point at all in thinking which song I would sing in the final, because there was simply no way I'd get through.

I didn't feel depressed at that thought though, because when I first joined Silver Spires, I never thought in a million years that I'd be able to sing solo and play a song I'd written in front of a huge audience without dying a thousand deaths. In fact, I didn't think I'd be able to do it even a few weeks ago. This competition had changed so much for me. Now that I knew I could go out and perform, I truly felt like a real musician, and that made me so happy. I was determined to play in school concerts at every opportunity from now on. And not only that, but I would also work hard at the classical music for my lessons, as well as writing more songs and playing pop music in my free time.

I was sitting on a high cloud looking up and down and all around at my lovely musical life.

Chapter Nine

Walking into the auditorium this second time was not half so scary as the first time. My heart was still racing, but a part of me actually wanted to get onto the stage, and that was a totally new feeling for me.

Georgie and the others gave me huge two-armed waves from where they were sitting. Their seats were much further back this time, but at least they were all together. As I went to join them, I noticed that there were even more teachers in the audience than there had been last Saturday. My eyes ran along the back three rows, where they were all sitting, and I spotted a few of the visiting music teachers amongst the others, including Mr. Wagstaffe. He caught my eye and gave me a little kind of salute, along with a big grin. I wondered if he thought it was strange that Mrs. Roach wasn't there to see me perform. It gave me a sinking feeling thinking about that. She'd made it perfectly clear what she thought about this trivial, fun concert.

"What number are you? When do you sing?" Georgie asked me urgently.

"I'm third," I replied, sucking my lips nervously and feeling myself tense up again.

"Don't do that," hissed Katy, pretending to be cross as she whipped out a lipgloss from her bag and passed it along to me.

The atmosphere in the auditorium was even more electric than the last time and you could tell that everyone was dying for the show to start. When the curtains opened and Miss York appeared, the most ginormous cheer went up.

"I think we're in for an incredibly exciting evening," she began. Then she rushed straight on to announce that Eve was first up, which set off another wave of clapping and cheering.

Eve went to the piano and adjusted the microphone slightly, then told us that her song was called "Hidden Codes". The last few shufflings and murmurings of the audience melted into silence and she began to sing.

I really loved her song. It was as quiet and gentle as my "goodbye" song, and I felt a rush of anxiety that maybe I was wrong to be attempting something more upbeat when I wasn't really that kind of person.

Or *was* I? It was weird, but when I sang now I somehow did feel like a different person from the old me. I'd noticed the change happening gradually during the last week. Even when I'd sung in front of Georgie and the others, I hadn't held back. And they'd said they liked it, hadn't they? In my mind I rewound back to the little practice room at Hazeldean and tried to remember the exact look on my friends' faces, because now I was worrying that they might have just been being kind.

I could feel my mouth getting dry, so I told myself to stop thinking about anything except the here and now and to try to enjoy Eve's song. Her piano-playing was brilliant. She's such a talented musician and the music she'd written for the accompaniment was really complicated.

Georgie whispered to me afterwards that she thought there should have been less piano and more singing and I immediately started worrying about the very opposite thing – maybe I should have had a piano solo in the middle of my own song, like Eve had done. Well, it was too late now.

The Craze's song was quite similar to the one they'd done before, but everyone clearly loved it, which got me all anxious for the tenth time that I shouldn't have changed my style, because if people voted for you it must be because they liked your original style. I sighed and sucked the shine off my lips again.

When my name was announced I don't know how I managed to get myself on the stage, I was in such a state. But somehow I did, and then I felt an idiot for having such a babyish title as "My Best Friend and Me", especially when I heard some older girls murmur, "Aah, sweet!"

But once I was playing the piano and I'd started singing, the same thing happened as when I'd performed it for my friends in the practice room. I felt the song kind of taking me over, and I didn't come back to reality for ages – in fact not until a sudden burst of clapping made me jump. It was the best sound in the world and was even lovelier than the week before because I thought it lasted longer.

I didn't care what happened after that. The other

bands were all so brilliant, and people stamped as well as cheered for Demonstrate and for Bella. Especially Demonstrate, which surprised me. I'd guessed Bella would get the biggest cheers, but her song didn't seem quite so popular as the one she did in the first round. I actually didn't think this second song was as good as her other one either, although I still loved it, because she's got such a beautiful voice and she's a great performer. In fact I couldn't help feeling sorry for Contemporary Counterpoint, who came after her, because their sound was much more classical and I didn't think the audience appreciated it as much.

When it was finally time for the vote, I was completely relaxed. It was my friends who were all wound up. "You're very calm, Mamma Mia," said Georgie.

"That's because I'm not bothered any more. I know I won't get through, but I'm just glad I've done it, and I'm definitely going to carry on singing and composing, whatever Mrs. Roach says!"

"Go Mia!" said Katy.

And the others laughed and agreed that I had a great attitude. But in fact I wasn't feeling quite so brave inside. If only I could make Mrs. Roach understand that I still love classical music and I always will, but composing and singing pop songs counts too. I sighed. I'd never be able to convince her. She was just too set in her ways.

I voted for Bella again, and as I was handing my voting card along the line, my phone vibrated and I saw that I had a text from Mum.

Dying 2 know – hows it going?

I texted back: *Just votin. Don't hold breath!*

When I'd pressed the send key, I glanced up and saw Bella was standing there.

"I adored your song, Mia!"

"Oh...thank you."

"In fact I voted for you!"

"Oh...well actually, I voted for you!"

"You have to be quite brave to write something in a completely different style, don't you?"

I nodded, knowing what she meant.

"What do you mean, 'brave'?" asked Katy, tuning in.

"Well, you know, if everyone loved what you did first time round, you kind of worry that they might not like it if you do something completely different, don't you?"

"So why did *you* do something different then?" Katy wanted to know.

But my phone vibrated just then and I was reading

Mum's reply, so I didn't hear how Bella answered.

Good luck with votes. Let me know.

Dad found that song by the way.

He's put CD in post. X

Something tightened up inside me like a gasp, and my face must have shown what I was feeling, because Georgie's arm was round me in a flash. "What? What's happened? You look awful!"

I glanced up and noticed Bella had gone, thank goodness. "Oh...nothing. I suddenly...felt a big rush of nerves, that's all."

Georgie laughed and patted me on the back. "No need for nerves when you get praise from the great goddess Bella, Mamma Mia!" Then she flopped back into her seat, staring fixedly at the closed curtains, and said, "Come on! I want to hear the votes!" When the curtains immediately began to open, the others all laughed as though Georgie had performed a magic trick, so no one noticed my straight face.

Miss York said she was about to announce the three successful acts, and my friends all held hands again. Georgie squeezed so tightly I had to ask her if she'd mind letting go a bit. I also reminded her that it was pointless doing any squeezing or praying or finger-crossing or anything, because there was no way I'd be voted through.

Miss York spoke in her best presenter's voice, as though she was on a reality TV show. "So the first act to go through to the final is..." The pause was making the audience break out in nervous giggles, and whenever one person giggled that set someone else off. "...Demonstrate!"

"I don't know how I'm going to bear all this tension!" I heard Grace tell Jess excitedly.

I shivered. *Me neither.* I couldn't get Mum's text out of my head. *Dad found that song by the way...*

She didn't text, *Dad thinks he's found that song.* No.

Miss York was about to announce another successful finalist. It felt as though my heartbeat was the only sound breaking the silence in the auditorium. I knew it would be Bella. But I couldn't work out in my mind how I should feel about that. I still didn't know for sure whether she'd cheated. And anyway, I hadn't even recognized her song this week...

"Next up..."

I made myself turn my brain off from all its confusing thoughts.

"Don't make us wait so long!" called out one of the teachers from the back. "We're all having heart attacks back here!"

The audience erupted with laughter.

"Okay, here it comes... Bella!"

And in a flash the laughter changed to an enormous cheer, but Miss York put her hand up and the cheer sank back into a tense silence. It had been obvious that Bella and Demonstrate would get through, but who would be the third act? Personally, I guessed The Craze. Of the remaining acts, they'd got the loudest cheer before.

Miss York scarcely paused for breath this time. "The last act to go through is...Mia Roberts!"

I gasped and felt tingles all over my whole body, but they were quickly crushed in Georgie's big hug. "Mia! You're such a star!" And as the clapping went on around me, I sat up on the highest cloud again, with nothing in my mind except how lucky and happy I was.

"So what are you going to sing for the final?" my friends asked excitedly in the interval.

I just needed to check that they all agreed with me. "Which one is better?" I asked them.

"The one you've just done!" they said.

And I nodded. I knew they were right.

Demonstrate, Bella and I had to go into the green room with Miss York. Mrs. Harrison, Mr. Ray and

Mam'zelle Clemence were there too. They all congratulated us on being in the final round, then Miss York reminded us that the winning act was to be entered for the audition to *Stars in the Wings*. "It's a huge honour," she said, smiling warmly. "Whoever gets chosen from Silver Spires will find themselves amongst the best singer/songwriters of your age in the whole of the UK."

"Well that would be you then, Bella!" said one of the Demonstrate girls. And while the others laughed, the anxious thoughts came rushing back through my head, no matter how much I tried to force them away because I so hated being wound up by them.

Bella shook her head modestly and said, "No, no, don't say that! It could be any of us!"

"Well, we'll soon see," said Miss York. "Now, let me just make a note of which songs you're all going to sing. You can either choose the same one you sang tonight, or go back to the one you did last week."

"We're going to do the same one," said one of the Demonstrate band members.

"Me too," I told Miss York and she wrote it down. Then I held my breath and crossed my fingers that Bella would also choose the one she'd sung tonight. That would mean I wouldn't have to worry any more. Surely it wouldn't matter that she'd cheated in the first round, as long as it wasn't that song that won her the audition for *Stars in the Wings*.

I watched her as she narrowed her eyes in thought. "Er...I think I'll go back to my other song," she said, and I felt an icy shiver run down my spine.

"Are you all right, Mia? You look a bit pale," said Mrs. Harrison.

"Yes, I'm fine!" I smiled and tried to look as bright and breezy as the words of my "friendship" song, but I couldn't make my anxiety go away, and I knew I'd never be able to sing such an upbeat song feeling like I did. "Actually, Miss York, could I change my mind about my song. I think I'd rather sing the one I sang last time."

"Are you sure, Mia?"

I nodded, and was aware of everyone looking at me.

"Okay, that's fine. Now, we've put your names in this tin and I'm going to ask Mrs. Harrison to pick out one of the bits of paper to see who's going to sing first..."

Mrs. Harrison unscrewed her piece of paper and read out, "Demonstrate!"

"Mr. Ray, would you do the honours now, please."

I waited tensely for Mr. Ray, and when he said,

"Bella!" my heart sank. I didn't want to sing straight after Bella. I really didn't.

"So, Mia, you're last." Miss York smiled. "Now you're all free to go and join your friends. And girls," she added, as we started to move towards the door, "you've been voted the most popular of all the acts, so just enjoy yourselves. No need to be nervous!"

We all thanked her and went off into the auditorium.

Of course, Georgie and the others wanted to know the order we were singing in, and they seemed to feel sorry for me having to wait till the end, but what I guessed they were really thinking was that the audience might lose interest after Bella. I was a bit nervous about what I had to say next, because I wasn't sure my friends were going to be very impressed, but I plucked up my courage. "Er...by the way, I decided to sing the 'goodbye' song."

"Oh no!" said Georgie.

"Why?" asked Naomi and Katy, at exactly the same moment.

"For a change," was all I could think of to say.

Georgie tipped her head to one side and gave me her fond-mother-getting-a-bit-impatient-now look. "You're mad!"

I knew she was right, but my mood had changed

too much. I'd never be able to sing an upbeat song now.

"No, I think it's fine," said Naomi. "Mia should sing whatever she feels like singing."

"But I don't get why you changed your mind," said Georgie.

I shrugged. "Just did."

"She's here! It's starting!" squeaked Katy, as the curtains opened and there stood Miss York.

First she checked that everyone had been given a second voting card. Then she told the audience the same thing she'd told us contestants in the green room, and it was obvious from the silence that everyone was very impressed with the thought of someone from Silver Spires trying out for such an important national concert. I found myself sinking into my seat as she talked, but then I shot back up again when Demonstrate went back onstage and began to sing, because it was so loud and had a really good beat. It was true that they were singing the same song as before, but it sounded completely different and I was really impressed with the way they must have got this second version ready in case they got through to the final. The audience actually stood up and started dancing – even some of the teachers.

Nobody moved a muscle when Bella sang though, because I suppose people had forgotten how beautiful her other song was. Her voice rang round the auditorium: *"I'm looking for the star that's going to show me how to get to you."* But inside my head all I could hear was, *You paint a golden circle round your dreams to keep them safe inside.* My insides knotted. I was more sure than ever that this was Dad's song. But I mustn't think about it. I mustn't.

When she finished, the audience rose to its feet. They loved her.

"Mia, you'll be brilliant," Georgie suddenly whispered. She must have noticed how stressed out I was and thought I was just nervous about singing after Bella. But it was so much more than that.

I walked as quickly as I could to the stage and the piano. My legs weren't shaking any more, but my mouth was dry. The tension and the nervousness had left my body and I just felt...flat. Yes, I think that was the word. I announced the title of my song, then started to sing it. It was coming out slower than usual and the words were almost catching in my throat, because the flatness was sinking into sadness. I was thinking about Mum and Dad, but not just about saying goodbye to them. I found I was actually imagining I'd had my scholarship taken away and, in my mind, the look on Mum's face was heartbreaking.

The moment I finished, I stood up, and tried to smile at the audience as they clapped. Then I left the stage, feeling quite relieved that I'd managed to get through the song, and that the whole thing would be over very soon. But the clapping went on for ages, and my flat spirits couldn't help buzzing and bubbling just a teeny bit.

"You were absolutely the best ever!" said Grace, leaning over Georgie as I sat down, and I stared at her as though she was crazy, because that really wasn't true.

"The best ever!" echoed Katy.

"Such a good idea singing the 'goodbye' song," said Naomi.

"The way you sang it was incredible," said Jess. "We all completely get why you decided to go back to that one now."

Georgie didn't say anything, but when I looked at her I saw she had tears in her eyes, and that moved me even more than what the others were saying. I felt a lump in my throat. Maybe I didn't want this contest to be over after all. Then Miss York was back onstage, telling us it was time to cast our final votes.

"You sounded so sad when you were singing," said Georgie. "Were you thinking about your mum and dad?"

I nodded. "I was thinking how upset they'd be if I had my scholarship taken away from me for not practising enough."

"Well, that's not going to happen," said Naomi, leaning across Georgie. "You've only had a little blip with your practice because of this contest. Surely Mrs. Roach will understand that. And anyway, Miss York is Head of Music and *she* thinks you're great!"

"Let's go outside for a bit," said Jess, "just while they count the votes."

So we did and it was lovely and cool and quiet. Georgie linked her arm through mine and sighed. "It's such a shame it's nearly all over. The Star contest has been totally fab."

"You've still got your play to come," I pointed out.

"I know. And I'm loving working on it, but there won't be the same atmosphere as this when we perform it, even though it'll be in the theatre."

"Why not?"

"I don't know. It's just not such a big thing as the Star contest. I mean, just think – whoever wins is going to get the chance to represent the school!"

I bit my lip.

"Are you nervous about the result, Mia?"

I shook my head. "No. I know Bella's going to win. I'm not thinking for a single second that it might be me." I'd spoken firmly and I meant what I'd said. But it was true, I was very nervous. If Bella won, what would I do? Should I tell someone about my suspicions? Who would I dare to tell?

Georgie didn't reply to what I said, just gave me a quick hug and then we all went back inside.

A couple of minutes later the curtains opened, and I had to go onstage with the other acts from the final. We each had a particular place to stand on the stage, and then I *did* feel a bit nervous, like a little girl again, surrounded by cool, glam, older, taller students. All the teachers who'd been involved with organizing the contest were on the stage too. And so was Ms. Carmichael, the Head of the whole school. She stepped forward and began to speak about what a wonderful event the Silver Spires Star contest had turned out to be. She said she'd been really impressed with all the acts, and that she'd had no idea there was so much talent in the school.

"But there can be only one winner and we've counted up the votes very carefully. Very, *very* carefully, because I can tell you it was an extremely close-run thing. So, without further ado, I'm going to tell you which act is the Silver Spires Star act, who will go on to represent our school in the auditions for the biggest national singer/songwriter show ever to be staged in the United Kingdom for under-fifteens. Our wonderfully deserving winner is...Bella!"

"Yesss!" came the jubilant cry from the audience and I felt the blood leave my face as I turned to look at Bella. She threw her head back as though she was thanking God as the applause erupted and raced and roared round the auditorium. The girls in Demonstrate all crowded round to hug her, and I felt as though I was in the middle of a strange dream as I took my turn. I don't know how I managed to keep the smile on my face, but I tried my very hardest because I didn't want anyone thinking I was in a sulk because I hadn't won.

In no time at all, Bella's friends came hurtling down from their places onto the stage to give her more hugs and pats on the back, and the teachers congratulated her, and gradually the contestants and the audience muddled up more and more, and the whole theatre throbbed with excited chatter and squeals of happiness.

But it looked as though Miss York wanted silence to say something, as she had stepped to the front of the stage and raised both her hands. A few people noticed and shushed the people next to them, then big shushing noises spread out all over the place until eventually we were all quiet.

"Sorry to interrupt your happy celebrations, everyone. We can carry on in a moment, but first I think we'd all like to hear from Bella!"

After another wave of cheering, Miss York took the microphone from its stand and turned to Bella. "I know you've not had much time to think about it, but have you decided, by any chance, which song you think you'd like to sing at the audition for *Stars in the Wings*?"

I wanted to block my ears or run away – anything to stop myself having to hear what Bella was about to say.

She pursed her lips and stared right out to the back of the auditorium as though she was considering her answer really carefully, and after a few seconds she quietly announced her decision. "'Is Anyone There?'"

"Yesss!" said a group of girls nearby, as though they'd been having a bet on it. As everyone laughed and Miss York thanked Bella and told us all to go back to our celebrations, my mind flooded with golden circles and dreams and the horrible question that wouldn't leave me alone, but that was so much more important to answer now that Bella would definitely be representing Silver Spires.

What if I found out for sure that she *had* cheated? What was I supposed to do?

Chapter Ten

On Monday morning I was first to wake up. Lemon sunlight was streaming into our dorm, because we hadn't shut the curtains when we'd gone to bed. I could see nothing but blue sky, and for about three seconds I felt completely happy, until I remembered that this was the day when Dad's CD would probably arrive in the post. Immediately I started to get into a state again. I looked at my watch. It was only six thirty. The others wouldn't be up for another half-hour.

I decided to get dressed and do some practice on my Debussy before breakfast, so I went down to one of the little practice rooms and took out my music. I'd worked on it a lot the day before, and found that all the time I was playing it I couldn't think about anything except the music because I had to concentrate so hard. It was the best possible escape from the big worry that wouldn't leave me alone, so I didn't stop practising and practising. I loved the Debussy now, and really hoped Mrs. Roach would be pleased with me on Thursday.

This morning I was determined to get right to the end of the piece if I could, and as soon as I'd played the first few notes, the music filled every corner of my mind and cleared out my thoughts about Dad's CD.

The thoughts came sailing back during breakfast though, and I couldn't keep my anxiety hidden from Georgie and the others.

"Don't worry, Mia. There'll probably be another contest next year," said Georgie.

The last thing I wanted was for my friends to think I was upset because I hadn't won the contest. That would be terrible. I just wanted to listen to Dad's CD and then I would know for sure one way or the other whether Bella had cheated. I was hoping and hoping that it would turn out that her tune had sometimes just sounded a bit like the one on the CD and that it was nothing more than that, so I could forget all about it and be happy for Bella. After all, she was easily the best performer and singer, so it would be good for Silver Spires if she auditioned for *Stars in the Wings*.

I don't know how I got through my first two lessons, but when the bell finally went for morning break I made an excuse about having to get my music and rushed back to Hazeldean. It felt so strange being in the boarding house at this time of morning during the week. The place was completely deserted, although I could hear a vacuum cleaner whirring away somewhere upstairs.

From the entrance hall, I crept round the corner to the corridor where our pigeonholes are. There were letters in several of them and, in mine, the dreaded parcel. I picked it up as though it was a bomb that might go off at any moment, and carried it carefully to the common room. Then, closing the door quietly behind me, I opened the parcel to find a Jed Jarrow CD and a little note from Dad.

Hi Mia,

I finally remembered what that song was you were singing to me. It's called "Circles" (track 3) and it is by Jed Jarrow. Turned out I'd not thrown it away after all. So here you are! Hope you enjoy it. Love Dad.

I took the CD out of its case with trembling fingers, put it in the CD player, pressed play on track three, and held my breath.

Immediately the room filled up with the music that I loved so much from our family days at home, but I didn't love it at that moment because an awful coldness was creeping around me. This was the exact music of Bella's song. She hadn't changed a single thing except the words. I stood there, feeling frozen and terrible. It wasn't as if the music was just a *bit* similar to hers, it was totally identical. There was no way she could represent Silver Spires in the *Stars in the Wings* auditions with this song. What if she got through? It would look as if the school had cheated. And that would be awful for Silver Spires. But what was I going to do? Who was I going to tell? How would I dare go to Miss York and say that I'd found Bella out? I didn't even want to tell Georgie. It would just seem like I was a nasty jealous person, who hated that Bella had won.

"Mia?"

I jumped with the shock of hearing the voice of our housemistress, Miss Carol, so close.

"Mia, what are you doing listening to music? Break time's over. You should be in lessons."

I stared at her, feeling my face losing its colour.

"I...I...was just..."

The song was still playing. Surely Miss Carol would recognize it in a moment. She'd definitely been at the concert both Saturdays. I stayed silent and watched her anxious face turn thoughtful. "Are you all right, Mia?"

"I...I'm not sure." The music seemed too loud for the room. I looked at Miss Carol and suddenly saw her face change as she listened. She closed her eyes slowly, then opened them again and nodded. Just one small brisk nod, as though she was telling herself to do something. The track ended and I pressed stop abruptly. "I was listening to my dad's CD," I managed to carry on. "He...sent it to me because I...remembered the music from when I was young and we used to sit round the fire at home..."

I knew I wasn't making any sense, but I was just babbling on because I couldn't quite make myself come to the truth. It felt like a betrayal.

"It's all right, Mia. We know."

"You know...what?"

"Mia, come along to my flat. Bring the CD case with you. I was going to talk to you later, but I think now would be better. Let's go and have a cup of tea."

* * *

Miss Carol sat opposite me in her living room. She'd made the tea while I'd been sitting on her settee, flipping through a pile of magazines and feeling for a few moments as though I was in a dentists' waiting room, about to have a nasty injection. She leaned forwards and looked at me carefully.

"I'll come straight to the point, Mia. Yesterday, we teachers had a meeting, because two or three members of staff had commented after the contest that they thought they recognized some of Bella's music…"

I swallowed. "You mean…the song she sang in the first round, and at the end?"

"Well actually it was the other song at first. It seems she took different bits from a couple of existing songs and stuck them together. But then Mrs. Harrison said that Mr. Wagstaffe had also recognized her *first* song. He'd not been at the first round of the contest, but he had a shock when he heard it at the final on Saturday, because it was clearly the same song as this one he knew, only with different words. So…you obviously recognized it too, Mia."

I nodded, feeling so relieved that Bella had already been found out and that I didn't have to be the one to betray her.

"Well, since our meeting, Miss York has spoken to Bella, and Bella has admitted that she did indeed borrow the melodies of those other songs. She's truly sorry for what she did and accepts that she can't possibly audition for *Stars in the Wings*."

I nodded again.

"And this is why I was going to speak to you, Mia. You see the person who came second in the final, with just three votes fewer than Bella, was you."

I nearly spilled my tea, I got such a shock. "Me? Are you sure you counted properly?"

Miss Carol laughed. "Well I didn't count the votes personally, Mia, but Miss York tells me there was definitely no mistake."

"Oh...right." I didn't know what to say.

"So what Miss York and myself and all the teachers want to know is...would you be happy to audition for *Stars in the Wings*?"

Then I *did* spill my tea. The mug just tipped as I was trying to put it back on the table. "Oh sorry, I..."

Miss Carol grabbed a tissue and wiped up the tea in a second. "That's nothing, Mia. The important thing is, would you be prepared to do it?"

My whole body suddenly filled with the most excited buzz, but then, just as quickly as it had come, the buzz disappeared. "But so many people voted for Bella. I'll just be a big disappointment to them. I know I will."

"No, I really don't think so, Mia. You see—"

There was a sudden knock at Miss Carol's door. "Sorry, Mia, I'll see if this is anything urgent..."

Miss Carol went to answer the door and I got a shock when she came back in with Georgie just behind her.

"Georgie was worried that you hadn't showed up for English," said Miss Carol. "Come on, you may as well join the party, Georgie, now you're here. I'll pour out another cup of tea."

A few minutes later Georgie knew everything. She'd been a bit cross that I hadn't said anything to her, but only a bit. Now she was more excited about the whole *Stars in the Wings* show.

"You're going to be a star!" she said grabbing my hands and staring at me, with big sparkling eyes. "And *I* know you!" she added, looking suddenly awestruck. "Can I have your autograph?"

Miss Carol laughed, but I didn't even manage a smile. "Nobody will want me to do it," I mumbled. "Bella was first choice. I'm sorry, I just don't want to do it, Miss Carol. I can't."

"Well I think everyone will be very disappointed

if you say no, Mia," said Miss Carol, looking concerned. "I mean, your parents, the teachers, your piano teacher... Everyone will want you to enter."

"Mrs. Roach won't," I said, trying not to sigh. "She'll be happy that I can get back to my proper practice."

"You're wrong there, Mia. Naturally, Miss York kept Mrs. Roach in the picture about what's been happening, and apparently Mrs. Roach had no idea you were quite so talented."

"She didn't think the Star contest was important at all," I said quietly.

"Well I think Miss York might have been singing your praises, Mia, because I can assure you that Mrs. Roach wants to support you in your singing and composing as much as she possibly can. In fact, she actually told Miss York she thought she'd been a bit short-sighted, because she had no idea that you had a serious talent as a singer/songwriter."

I sank back into the settee, feeling one big pressure sliding off my shoulders. But there was still no way I could audition for *Stars in the Wings* and I knew my other worry was showing on my face, because Georgie frowned at me with big concentration as she leaned forwards and spoke carefully to Miss Carol.

"Do Bella's friends know she cheated?"

"I'm afraid they do, yes. Her dorm mates wanted to know why she was crying and she told them. Unfortunately for her, I should think the whole of Year Eight probably knows by now."

I felt myself tensing up. Poor Bella.

Miss Carol tipped her head to one side and gave me a sympathetic smile. "After summer it'll all be forgotten, Mia. Bella is a popular girl. Her friends will forgive her. It's nothing for you to worry about."

"Please say you'll try out for *Stars in the Wings*, Mia…" said Georgie, coming right up to my face with praying hands.

I shook my head. "No. I just can't."

Miss Carol was right about everyone finding out that Bella had cheated, because at lunchtime there seemed to be no other topic of conversation in the dining hall. The whole place was buzzing with the shocking news.

"Who's going to represent the school now?" I heard a Year Nine girl say, as I stood in the lunch queue near her table with my tray.

Then someone from the same table must have spotted me and called out, "Hey, Mia, was it you or Demonstrate who came second?"

I bit my lip. "Er...I think it was me."

Georgie was right behind me. "It *was* Mia!" she said firmly. "All the teachers want Mia to sing for *Stars in the Wings* but she's got this stupid idea in her head that she didn't win and she hasn't got any right to do it!" Georgie rolled her eyes dramatically. "Can you believe it?"

The queue had shuffled forwards and I quickly moved on with it. I didn't want to be a part of this conversation any more, because it was obvious nobody would want little me in Bella's place.

By the time I'd got my lunch and sat down with the others, there was no sign of Georgie. I glanced over at the table where the Year Nine girls were and saw that they'd gone too, which puzzled me.

"Hey, Mia!" called out a Year Seven named Bryony, from two tables away. "Naomi says you're not going to do *Stars in the Wings*. Are you mad or something?"

"Did you come second then, Mia?" asked a friend of Bryony's.

"Yes she did!" Katy answered for me. She must have been able to see that I was getting embarrassed.

"You're brilliant, Mia!" said someone else from Bryony's table. "You've *got* to do it."

It was kind of Bryony and her friends to stick up for me, but they were only Year Seven. The older students wouldn't want me representing Silver Spires, I just knew it.

"Ssh!" Bryony said to her friend. "Ms. Carmichael."

I looked towards the door. Sure enough, Ms. Carmichael had come in with Miss York, and just behind her were the Year Nine girls who'd been talking to Georgie. And then, there was Georgie herself. The whole dining room went quiet. It wasn't just that Ms. Carmichael was there – she often came in. It was the fact that there was something going on. She was whispering to Miss York and looking around the room. Then her eyes alighted on me, as Georgie came nipping over and squashed herself in between me and Katy.

"What's happening?" I whispered.

"Nothing," she answered, trying to look innocent.

But a second later there was complete silence, because Ms. Carmichael had rung a little bell.

"Girls, I'm sorry to interrupt your lunch but I wanted a quick word with you, and I want it now, while our Star contest is still fresh in your minds. I think most of you, if not all of you, will know by now that sadly the songs Bella sang in the contest were not her own material. As we cannot tolerate cheating or deception such as this here at Silver Spires, I'm afraid we have taken the decision that it would be best for Bella to be sent home for the last week of term. Bella has apologized and is most repentant, and next term will be a clean slate for her, because she's a lovely, talented girl who simply made a mistake – one that she won't ever make again." She paused, letting her eyes travel round the silent room.

"In the meantime, we have a problem on our hands, because in second place in our contest, by a very narrow margin, was Mia Roberts..."

All heads seemed to turn to look for me, and a second later I was sure my face was bright pink, because I could sense so many pairs of eyes on me.

"Hey!" said a few girls nearby, breaking into applause, and I noticed the Demonstrate girls amongst them. "Go Mia!"

And then it was like fire spreading round the hall, and I couldn't help feeling tingles of happiness, even though I was still embarrassed.

Ms. Carmichael carried on talking. "The problem is that Mia doesn't feel that she deserves to enter

Stars in the Wings and has told us that she doesn't want to do it…"

One of the Year Tens was suddenly on her feet. "Mia, you've got to do it. You were the best!"

"I was second," I quickly pointed out.

"You were *the best*," the Year Ten girl came straight back at me. Then her voice softened. "Because you wrote your own songs, Mia."

A huge cheer went up all over the dining hall and then everyone was stamping and banging their fists on the tables and chanting, "Mi-a, Mi-a, Mi-a, Mi-a…"

"There!" said Georgie, putting her arm round me and whispering right into my ear, because it was impossible to hear a thing with so much noise going on all around me. "*Now* will you believe me?"

I looked up at Ms. Carmichael and saw that she was smiling at me with raised eyebrows. "Well?" she mouthed.

I stood up slowly, feeling my heart beat with excitement and happiness, and instantly there was silence again.

"Thank you," I said quietly. "I'm convinced now that you want me to do it…so I will."

Then there was another burst of cheering and clapping and stamping and Miss York actually came over and gave me a big hug. Everyone was crowding around me, but Georgie put her hands up like a policeman stopping the traffic. "Give her a bit of space, people!" she said, pretending to be bossy. "I'm her manager, you know, and I'm not having her crushed like this!"

I'd never felt so popular in my whole life. Or so happy. I couldn't wait to tell Mum and Dad.

The sun was so bright as Georgie and the rest of my dormies and I left the dining room and made our way over to afternoon lessons. My eyes went straight to the tall spires of the main building. They shone as brightly as real silver and glinted and sparkled like everlasting fireworks.

"Look!" I whispered.

Everyone followed my gaze.

"Aren't we lucky?" said Naomi.

No one replied, but I knew we were all agreeing with her in our minds. It was just a beautiful moment that we didn't want to disturb by speaking out loud.

Beside me, Georgie reached for my hand and I saw that her eyes were sparkling.

"Yes," she said, breaking the silence. "We must be the luckiest girls in the world."

I smiled at her and thought, *Yes, and I must be the very luckiest of all because I truly* am *a real musician.*
And that's all I've ever wanted to be.

School Friends Fun!

Performing in the Silver Spires Star Contest was something I thought I'd never be able to do! But with the help of my lovely friends, I actually learned to enjoy singing in front of people. And you can too!

How to give a star performance!

Stage fright can creep up on everyone, even superstars. And it doesn't matter what sort of performance you're giving, a little confidence boost can make all the difference. So, if you've got your eyes on singing stardom, like me, here's some fun ideas to try out with *your* friends!

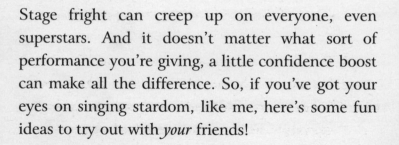

★ Whether you're going solo or forming a band it's important to get your sound spot-on. Spend time listening to different types of music before settling on a song that suits your voice and ability. Don't be afraid to experiment and swap tunes with your friends for inspiration.

★ Grab a video camera and record each other's performances. Watching yourself on tape can be cringe-worthy, but you'll be able to see what you're doing right, and where you need a bit more practice.

★ Get your friends together for a pop party! Dress up like your fave pop princess or girl group, perfect those dance moves and practise singing like divas. Even the top pop stars started out by practising in front of the mirror with a hairbrush...

★ Katy's cool makeover really boosted my confidence, so why not do the same with your friends? Borrow each other's clothes or try a funky hairstyle for a totally fresh look. Just remember, you'll feel more confident if your new style still expresses who you are, so don't do anything too drastic!

So what are you waiting for? Grab your friends and have some School Friends fun!

Mia x

Complete your

School Friends

collection!

First Term at Silver Spires   9780746072240

Katy's nervous about going to boarding school for the
first time – especially with the big secret she has to hide.

Drama at Silver Spires   9780746072257

Georgie's desperate to get her favourite part in the school
play, but she's up against some stiff competition.

Rivalry at Silver Spires   9780746072264

Grace is eager to win in the swimming gala for Hazeldean
– until someone starts sending mean messages about her.

Princess at Silver Spires   9780746089576

Naomi hates being the centre of attention, but when she's
asked to model for a charity fashion show, she can't say no.

Secrets at Silver Spires   9780746089583

Jess is struggling with her schoolwork and has to have special
classes, but she can't bear to tell her friends the truth.

Star of Silver Spires   9780746089590

Mia longs to enter a song she's written in the Silver Spires
Star contest, but she's far too scared to perform onstage.

So now that you know all about the
gang from Hazeldean's Amethyst dorm,
fancy meeting some of their
Forest Ash friends?

Look out for more **School Friends** stories,
featuring the Emerald dorm girls,
coming soon!

And don't forget, you can stay up-to-date
with all the Silver Spires news, plus try
a quiz to discover which School Friend
you're most like, at

www.silverspiresschool.co.uk

Check it out now!

Ann Bryant's School Days

Who was your favourite teacher?

At primary it was Mr. Perks – we called him Perksy. I was in his class in Year Six, and most days he let me work on a play I was writing! At secondary, my fave teacher was Mrs. Rowe, simply because I loved her subject (French) and she was so young and pretty and slim and chic and it was great seeing what new clothes she'd be wearing.

What were your best and worst lessons?

My brain doesn't process history, geography or science and I hated cookery, so those were my least favourite subjects. But I was good at English, music, French and P.E., so I loved those. I also enjoyed art, although I was completely rubbish at it!

What was your school uniform like?

We had to wear a white shirt with a navy blue tie and sweater, and a navy skirt, but there was actually a wide variety of styles allowed – I was a very small person and liked pencil-thin skirts. We all rolled them over and over at the waist!

Did you take part in after-school activities?

Well I loved just hanging out with my friends, but most of all I loved ballet and went to extra classes in Manchester after school.

Did you have any pets while you were at school?

My parents weren't animal lovers so we were only allowed a goldfish! But since I had my two daughters, we've had loads – two cats, two guinea pigs, two rabbits, two hamsters and two goldfish.

What was your most embarrassing moment?

When I was in Year Seven I had to play piano for assembly. It was April Fool's Day and the piano wouldn't work (it turned out that someone had put a book in the back). I couldn't bring myself to stand up and investigate because that would draw attention to me, so I sat there with my hands on the keys wishing to die, until the Deputy Head came and rescued me!

To find out more about Ann Bryant visit her website: www.annbryant.co.uk

If you like *School Friends*, you'll also love...

SUMMER CAMP SECRETS
by Melissa J. Morgan

MISS MANHATTAN
ISBN 9780746084557
City chick Natalie is surprised to find that she actually enjoys summer camp – until her big secret gets out...

PRANKSTER QUEEN
ISBN 9780746084564
Mischievous Jenna is famous for her wild stunts, but this year she's totally out of control. What's bugging her?

BEST FRIENDS?
ISBN 9780746084571
Fun-loving Grace starts hanging out with Gaby from rival bunk 3C, before she realizes what a bully Gaby can be.

LITTLE MISS NOT-SO-PERFECT
ISBN 9780746084588
Sporty, reliable Alex seems like the perfect camper. But she's hiding a problem that she can't bear to admit.

BLOGGING BUDDIES
ISBN 9780746084601
The girls are back home and keeping in touch through their camp blog. But one bunkmate needs some extra support.

PARTY TIME!
ISBN 9780746084618
Everyone's excited about the camp reunion in New York! But when it gets to party time, will the girls still get on?

THREE'S A CROWD

ISBN 9780746093382

New camper Tori is from LA and is just as super-hip as Natalie. Good thing Nat isn't the jealous type – or is she?

WISH YOU WEREN'T HERE

ISBN 9780746093399

Sarah stresses when classmate Abby turns up at camp – will she expose Sarah as a geek to all her fun-loving friends?

JUST FRIENDS?

ISBN 9780746093405

Priya's best friend is a boy but she's sure she could never have a crush on him – until he starts to like another girl...

JUST MY LUCK

ISBN 9780746093412

When practical jokes start happening during Colour War, Jenna is the obvious suspect. But could someone else be to blame?

FALLING IN LIKE

ISBN 9780746093429

Valerie's wicked stepsister, Tori's forbidden crush, Alyssa's censored artwork...life back home after camp is so complicated!

ON THIN ICE

ISBN 9780746093436

Tori's only allowed to invite five friends on her fab holiday weekend. But how can she choose without hurting anyone?

All priced at £4.99

www.summercampsecrets.co.uk

For more fun and
friendship-packed reads
check out
www.fiction.usborne.com